THE SOLDIER

A BRATVA ROMANCE

RENEE ROSE

BURNING DESIRES

Published in the United States of America

Wilrose Dream Ventures LLC

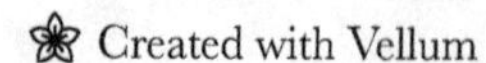

WANT FREE RENEE ROSE BOOKS?

Go to http://subscribepage.com/alphastemp to sign up for Renee Rose's newsletter and receive a free copy of *Alpha's Temptation, Theirs to Protect, Owned by the Marine, Theirs to Punish, The Alpha's Punishment, Disobedience at the*

Dressmaker's and *Her Billionaire Boss*. In addition to the free stories, you will also get bonus epilogues, special pricing, exclusive previews and news of new releases.

1

Pavel

I wrap my tattooed fingers under the deadbeat's jaw and trace a knife blade across his throat. "Don't make bets you can't cover," I tell him. I sharpened the blade before we came, so just the tickle of it cuts his skin and sends a trickle of blood down his fat neck. Enough to scare him if he's squeamish. We're not here to maim the guy, just to make him piss his pants.

Nikolai, our bookie, stands close, arms folded over his chest in clear condemnation. Beside him, Oleg, the enormous, silent enforcer, cracks his tattooed knuckles.

He already worked the asshole over pretty well. The guy will be bruised and swollen for a couple weeks, for sure. That's what happens when you fuck with the Chicago Bratva.

"Please. I'll get you the money. I swear." He's blubbering now. It didn't take long to break him, but it was still more time than I wanted to waste here.

Not that my job is a waste of my time. I'm damn lucky to be part of Ravil's bratva cell.

It's just that I have someone else to torture after this. Someone far more delectable and willing. But unfortunately, she lives in a different city, which means I have a flight to catch.

I meet Nikolai's eye, and he shrugs, leaving the call up to me.

I clean the blade of my knife on the *mudak's* shirt. "You have two weeks. Pay up or we take everything you love. Understand?"

"I understand," he moans. "I'll get you the money. I promise."

"You *had* the money," I remind him. "And instead of bringing it to us, you used it to place a new bet with the Tacones."

The guy hangs his head. "I know," he moans.

"So I'm telling you—we get paid first."

"I will—I will pay you first. I promise."

"Don't think you're welcome at my table again," Nikolai says. He takes it personally when players choose to sit with the Italians instead of us. The Tacones aren't our enemies; we have a tacit agreement to stick to our own specialties when it comes to organized crime in this city. Which means our poker games shouldn't overlap.

I lift my chin at Oleg, who takes one last swing at the guy's face for good measure, and then I cut the ropes tying him to the chair. He starts to scramble up, but I point the blade of my knife at his left eyeball, and he freezes.

"Sit. Count to four hundred. Then you leave."

"Four hundred. Got it. Four hundred," the guy babbles.

I pick up my jacket and pull it on as we leave the abandoned warehouse we chose for our little torture session. Pea gravel crunches underfoot as we walk to Oleg's SUV.

"Not up to your usual quality," Nikolai remarks as we walk. "You losing your taste for torture?"

"No." I don't tell him my tastes have just changed. I've found a far healthier outlet for my sadistic urges. I don't tell him, but he probably already knows. I live with these guys full time. It's pretty hard to keep secrets although we just found out Oleg kept a huge one about his past from us.

"Seriously, dude. I almost stepped in to throw a couple punches myself." Nikolai's still giving me shit.

I glance at Oleg, because the guy communicates more these days, and he shrugs and makes his fist nod, sign language for *yes*.

"*Da poshel ty.*" I tell them to go to hell.

We climb into Oleg's vehicle, and he starts it up to drive us back.

"Ravil's going to replace you if you don't start pulling your weight." Nikolai says it lightly, but a prickle on the back of my neck tells me to pay attention. I'm not sure if he's just trying to get a rise out of me or if he means it. Ravil is our *pakhan*, the boss of the Chicago bratva. The idea that he might be dissatisfied with my service puts me on edge. I'm lucky as hell to have this position, and I'm ambitious. I definitely hope to solidify my place for as long as I'm here. That way, hopefully, when I go back to Moscow, I'll have improved my position in the organization there.

"What the fuck are you talking about?" I snap.

Nikolai twists from the front seat to look at me. "He made a comment this morning about you leaving for the weekend again. Something about you not clearing it with him."

Blyad'. I hadn't cleared it with him. But I thought everyone knew I was going to L.A. for the weekend. I've gone every weekend since Valentine's, when Ravil sent me to a BDSM club on business, and I ended up claiming my little slave.

Still, assuming everyone knew I was going isn't the same thing as asking permission from the boss. I should've thought to ask for his leave, but we're not exactly timeclock employees. Our job descriptions are pretty loose. Basically, I do whatever the fuck Ravil tells me to do—legal or not.

Ravil owns me, but I'd do anything for him.

I scrub a hand over my face. "Okay. Thanks for telling me." Nikolai may come off as a dick, but I know he's trying to save my ass.

"What is your plan with this girl?" Nikolai asks.

I don't answer. It's none of his fucking business.

"You gonna keep this long-distance thing up permanently?"

"Nah," I say, trying to make it sound casual. Like breaking things off with Kayla is going to be easy for me.

The truth is, it's not. I know I'm a piece of shit for claiming her and keeping her as mine for the past month. Kayla has a life. A bright future. One that will only be hurt by association with me. And that's not even taking into consideration the emotional pain I'm going to cause her. Every week I let this go on makes it harder to break things off.

I should rip off the Band-aid now, before she gets even more bonded to me as her master than she already is.

Yeah, I'll break things off this weekend. Not when I get there but at the end. After we have enjoyed ourselves. I'll make sure she has the best orgasms of her life, and then I'll let her down gently. Blame it on the distance.

Oleg parks in the underground lot beneath the building Ravil owns across from Lake Michigan. The neighborhood calls it the Kremlin because he only lets Russians live and work here. Russians and his American bride. Also now

Oleg's new girlfriend, Story. For a brief moment, the thought of demanding my slave move here to Chicago, of installing her in the Kremlin so I can dominate her twenty-four/seven, flashes through my mind.

But of course, I would never do such a thing. She's an actress trying to make it in Los Angeles. Convincing her to move—and I'm not certain I could, even as willing as she is to do my bidding—would effectively terminate her dreams. I may be a selfish prick, but I'm not that big of an asshole.

I get out and check my phone. My suitcase is already packed and in my car. If I climb in now and drive straight to the airport, I'll get there in perfect time.

But Ravil. The last thing I need is my ass handed to me by the boss. Not after I've worked so hard to make myself indispensable.

Blyad.' I follow Nikolai and Oleg to the elevator and take it up to the top floor, where we all share the boss' penthouse. He stands at the giant floor-to-ceiling windows that look out over the lake, holding Benjamin, his five-month-old baby against his chest. He's murmuring softly to the baby in Russian.

Not a good time to interrupt.

But I don't have time to spare.

I go stand next to him, remaining quiet and looking out at the lake.

"What happened?" Ravil almost always speaks to us in English. When I moved here from Russia to join his cell, I didn't speak a word. This was how he made sure we learned—by forbidding our mother tongue until we were fluent in English.

"Nothing. We took care of it."

He slides a speculative look my way, but says nothing. Ravil is mild-mannered. Cool-tempered. Smart as hell. Not a man you should ever underestimate or cross. I'm fortunate he gave me a place here when I had to leave Moscow. I've tried to learn everything I can from him, emulate his ways. I'm rough around the edges, but growing more sophisticated every day.

I shove my hands in my pockets. Apologizing doesn't come easy to me. I can't think of the last time I did, actually. But I owe Ravil mad respect. "I should have asked your permission to leave town," I say, my gaze dropping to the face of his cherubic infant as the baby's eyelids flutter closed.

"Yes," Ravil agrees.

Fuck. Nikolai was right. I owe him big time for telling me.

"I'm sorry."

"Forgiven." He says it easily, while still making it clear my transgression required forgiveness.

I take a breath but can't think what to say next. Do I ask for belated permission? Maybe I should, but I can't bring myself to even offer the possibility of me *not* going. I have a slice of pure heaven waiting for me in California, and I intend to suck all the juice out of it before I break things off.

I start to tell him this is my last trip, but I can't make that promise, either.

"You're figuring things out." Ravil speaks for me.

For some inexplicable reason, my heart starts thudding. Ravil just spoke aloud what I've been pretending to myself I had already decided.

But what is there to sort out? Kayla is in Los Angeles. I'm here. What's more, I have plans to go back to Russia when things cool down. I've saved my money to start my own enterprise there. Not going back isn't an option—my mother is all alone there.

But he's right—I clearly haven't made my mind up yet,

or I wouldn't be going this weekend. My one-month arrangement with Kayla was over last week.

"Yes," I agree.

"Let me know when you do." He turns and walks away, leaving me sweating.

Fuck.

Another reason to conclude my adventure with Kayla this weekend.

And yet as I walk out the door to head for the airport, I'm almost certain I won't.

~

Kayla

I sip champagne in the lobby of the Four Seasons Beverly Hills, positioned just inside the front doors, so I can be seen by everyone who comes in. I'm in character, playing my part, so I ignore the notion that I don't belong here. That this place is for the rich and famous, and I'm just a wanna-be actress from Wisconsin.

I haven't seen anyone famous come in yet, but it occurs to me that hanging out here might be a strategy to get "discovered." You never know, right? That's what we tell ourselves, anyway. Me and my roommates and the rest of the unemployed actors in L.A.

My phone rings, and I pull it out of my purse, swiping across the screen when I see it's my agent.

"Hi, Lara."

"Kayla, listen, clear your schedule for this weekend. I might be able to get you an audition. I'm working on it."

This weekend. *Fuck.*

On weekends, I now belong to Pavel. But this is my career. It has to come first. "Yeah, okay," I tell her breathlessly. "What's it for?"

"It's a new television series directed by Blake Ensign, and I think you'd be perfect for one of the parts. Oh—I have to take this call. I'll talk to you soon." Lara ends the call in her typical important-agent fashion, even though she's not that important. She's definitely not the agent to the A-listers. Or even the B-listers. Otherwise, she wouldn't be my agent, would she?

But, whatever. I'm lucky I have an agent. It's more than most could say.

I sigh and put my phone back in my purse and drink some more champagne to calm my nerves. Pavel, my bad-boy Russian dom, will understand about tomorrow—if the audition even happens.

At least I think he will. The truth is, he may be my dom, we may do the most intimate of things each mind-blowing weekend, but we're still strangers. I say *dom*—not *boyfriend*—because there's nothing "boy" about Pavel, even though he's probably the same age I am. And no, I don't know his real age. There are a million things I don't know about Pavel. Like what he actually does for a living. Or what made him a sadist—if such things can be defined. They probably can't. I don't know what made me a submissive. I just know it turns me on more than all the love-making I experienced before I went to Black Light.

Just the thought of the things he'll do to me tonight sends a shiver up my spine.

I'm in a black cocktail dress—not as slinky or sexy as I'd like, but it has a built-in collar and an open cutout for my cleavage, which I think is hot. I hope Pavel feels the same way.

I recross my legs. I'm wearing fancy black thigh-highs, the kind with the seam that runs up the back and ends with a tiny satin bow a few inches from my ass. I changed my outfit fifteen times trying to get it right, and I'm still unsure about my choice. I feel slightly like a call-girl waiting for her john. Which is hot in a cosplay kind of way, but it might be a little too close to the truth.

Not that Pavel pays me. The first weekend he flew out to see me—the weekend after we were paired at Black Light, an exclusive BDSM club where we met, he held up a wad of bills before we parted. "This is not payment," he said in his sexy accent. He manages to be stern and commanding, even when giving me a gift. "Don't think that for even a second. This is spending money because I won't be around to take you out the rest of the week."

I only blinked twice before I took the money, accepting it with Pavel's kiss to my temple. I'm barely scraping by as a bit-part and commercials actress who does party promotions and light bartending to pay the rent. I'd like to be plucky and proud and tell him I don't need his money, but I'm really not that person. I'm definitely the "tend and befriend" kind of survivor. Which means I accept help when it comes. When I'd unrolled the bills later at home, I'd been shocked to find it wasn't a few twenties. It was a wad of hundreds—nine to be exact.

He repeated that the next three weekends we were together, slipping large amounts of money into my purse or pressing them into my hand. "*Not payment,*" he would say sternly in that sexy Russian accent, daring me to contradict him.

A bolt of excitement strikes like lightning the moment he walks through the glass doors. Power radiates from the man, contradicting his youth and street tattoos. His neatly trimmed beard adorns a square jaw and chin with a dimple in the center. He would be Hollywood handsome except for the distinct air of danger around him. More than one head turns to see who is coming in. It's L.A., so there are famous people everywhere—especially at the Four Seasons, and Pavel looks like he's one of them.

Like always, he's wearing expensive clothes, but his crisp button-down shirt is open at the throat, revealing the tattoos that crawl up his chest to his neck. He is every inch the bratva badass. He carries a small suitcase, which I know from experience contains his implements of torture. Things he will use to master me over and over again, all weekend long.

I slide forward on the modern couch, ready to surge to my feet, but he gives a minuscule shake of his head, his gaze bouncing off me to the line at the front desk.

The explosion of butterflies in my belly makes it hard to think. To decipher. Other than lifting one finger for a half-second, as if to signal me to wait, he doesn't acknowledge me. He walks past to stand in the line at the front desk. A hot flush floods my cheeks as I sit, my spine straight, tits out, awaiting his command.

I try to push back the pain of his rejection. It's not rejection. This is a test in obedience. How well do I read his wishes? How good am I at delayed gratification? He's edging me. That must be it.

Everything the man says or does sends flutters through me. His words are delicious, fantasy-inducing commands. His expressions tend to be dark, bordering on slight disapproval. He'll give me a flick of his eyebrow, a warning look. He plays the part of my forbidding master to a tee. Except I'm not even sure it's a part he's playing. All of our interactions are movie-worthy scenes, but I don't think this role is very far off from who he really is.

The problem is, I just don't know. Sometimes I'm not sure I want to know. We're playing out our fantasies with each other. Why would we want any part of real life in this?

One of the hotel staff brings him a tray with filled champagne glasses. He shakes his head but says something to the man then points in my direction. My hurt fades. He's still looking out for me, as a good master should. I'm offered more champagne, and I accept, not because I want it but because Pavel had it sent over to me.

He checks in and then strides over. This time I don't start to get up until I'm sure. Not until he holds out his hand for me. He's still cool and impassive. No expression whatsoever on the harsh planes of his face. I can't tell if he's happy to see me. If he's pleased or displeased with my outfit or the way I waited obediently. I set the champagne glass down. I don't need any more—one drink is plenty for a lightweight like me.

My hand is clammy in his as he helps me to my feet. He doesn't say a word. No kiss. No *how are you?* Or *You look great*. Nothing. He's all business. He drops his suitcase on top of mine, takes my hand again, and leads me to the bank of elevators, rolling both our suitcases with his free hand.

The butterflies become a hurricane, spiraling in frantic flight. I don't understand him and my need to please—to play this game properly—has me on a knife's edge.

We step into the elevator, and the doors shut. The moment we're alone, Pavel turns to me. One hand wraps in my hair, the other on my ass as he pushes me back against the elevator wall. His mouth descends on mine in a demanding kiss. His erection prods my belly, and his tongue sweeps into my mouth. Relief pours through me.

He's not dissatisfied. He *does* want me.

I wind my arms around his neck and kiss him back, wrapping one leg around his to draw him closer. We kiss like the world's about to end. Like if we don't devour each other's mouths, we'll never see the light of day again. It's only been a week since we've seen each other, and it feels like both yesterday and forever ago.

The elevator dings, and Pavel catches my hand, not looking at me as he leads me out, expertly maneuvering our stacked suitcases down the hall to a door, which he opens with his keycard.

He still hasn't spoken. I guess I haven't, either, because I'm waiting for him to lead. He's the master. I'm his slave. At least that's the game we've been playing since we met just over a month ago. He kicks the door shut and resumes our kiss with the same ferocity he left off. My butt hits the wall. The hard lines of his body mold against mine, demanding my yield. I surrender to him. To his skill. His domination, his lead. He catches my thigh and hikes it up, finding the top band of my thigh-highs.

"Hot," he breathes against my lips. For a first word, it seems appropriate. He strokes my ass, his palm sliding under the hem off the dress. "You look so fucking hot."

There. That's what I was hoping for. Why I changed my clothes over a dozen times.

He kisses down my neck as he palms my pussy like he owns it. Which he does. Consensually given, of course. Like always, I'm soft putty in his hands—quivering, ready, awaiting his command.

He doesn't give one. Instead, he just takes. He slides his fingers inside my panties and strokes over my slit. "Already wet." His neatly-trimmed beard tickles my ear. His Russian accent is thick—it always grows stronger when he's turned on. "Such a good girl. Ready to take my cock the moment I want to give it to you."

A shudder of pleasure goes through me at his dirty talk, and I drink up his praise, even though my state of readiness isn't something I have control over.

"Yes, sir," I pant.

"I need to be inside you, blossom," he says gruffly, rushing to free his erection.

Blossom. I love his pet name. It started because he thought I was too delicate a flower. Too crushable. We were paired by a roll of the roulette wheel at Black Light, and I think he was disappointed to get me. But when he found I took everything he dished—pain and humiliation alike—his disdain for me slowly turned to appreciation. After he broke me, when I humiliatingly lost my shit in a puddle of sub-drop sobs, he declared I belonged to him.

That was five weeks ago.

I don't help him now because my job is to submit. He drives the train.

He pulls my panties to the side and lines the head of his cock up with my entrance, bending his knees to lower to my height. We don't use a condom because I'm on the pill, we're monogamous, and we've both been tested and are clean. When he shoves in and up, he lifts me to my toes, sliding my hips up the wall.

I cry out, clutching his bulging biceps for stability.

"Whose pussy is this?" Pavel's fingers are rough on my ass as he helps lift me to the right height to nail me against the wall.

"Yours, Master!"

He thrusts in hard and fast. My back bangs against the wall. It's rough and frightening and wonderful. I lift my other leg to wrap around his waist, and he grinds into me, shoving in with each powerful snap of his hips. His teeth score my neck, he sucks and nips as he pounds into me.

I listen to the quickening of his breath. I will come the moment he does—if he allows it. I don't even think or try—it's like my body knows its master. It wants to join him in the release.

Pavel's strokes get harder, driving my body further up

the wall. I let out a cry of need. His breath catches, and he slams in deep. "Come." His command is strangled and guttural as he speaks over his own orgasm.

I relinquish all effort to hold back the squeezing of my muscles around his cock. There is nothing but the sound of his rasping breath, and the sensation of his cock pulsing inside me.

Pavel kisses my temple, my cheekbone, the bridge of my nose. These are the moments I savor. When I'm certain I've won his approval. When he's grateful and gentle and generous with the affection he otherwise holds back. "I needed that." He squeezes my ass and kisses my neck. "I couldn't even look at you in that dress when I came in; I knew I'd have the world's most visible boner walking to the front desk."

"Ah, that's what it was." I almost laugh with relief. "I thought you were playing some mindfuck to keep me off balance."

Pavel pulls back, easing out of me, and studies my face. He tucks his cock away and straightens my dress. "I hurt your feelings."

I shrug. He's great at reading me when he seeks an answer but is sometimes clueless about what to ask. My friend Sasha, who hooked us up, thinks I'm the first and only girlfriend he's ever had.

And I don't even consider myself his girlfriend.

What we have is something else.

I nod, and he strokes his thumb down my cheek.

"I'm into delivering physical pain not emotional, Kayla. I don't do mindfucks. I don't want you off-balance, I want you sure of me. Otherwise, how will you trust me with this fuck-hot body of yours?"

The flutters in my belly tumble once then settle down.

Pavel holds my jaw and hovers his lips above mine.

"I'm sorry, blossom. I'm a selfish prick. I didn't mean to hurt you." He kisses me so softly it almost makes me weep. It's the opposite of the hard, claiming kisses of the elevator. Something different. "Thank you for telling me. I won't leave you hanging again."

Everything in my chest goes warm and gooey. This is how things always are with Pavel. I'm on edge, a shivering, volatile mess, trembling for his attention, dying for affirmation, and then when he gives it to me, I soar like a kite.

My housemates think it's dysfunctional, but they don't understand BDSM. I think Pavel's the most exciting thing to ever happen to me.

2

Pavel

Kayla's knees buckle, and I catch her elbow to steady her. She's so fucking sweet. Definitely tender, like a little flower.

A flower I always fear I will crush.

How in the hell would I know that checking in first would crack her confidence? It's exactly this tenderheartedness that made me reject her when we first met at Black Light. I didn't think she'd last one minute with me without screaming *red*. But she proved me wrong.

Kayla will take just about everything I dish out without complaint. Those big blue eyes are always on my face, looking for my approval, for my next command. She's actually a dream submissive. But being her dom means I have to figure out the emotional shit, which isn't my forte.

Understatement.

I slide my lips over hers in a soft kiss, then trace the cutout of her dress with the tip of my index finger. "You look so beautiful, little flower. I should take you out for dinner and show you off, is that what you want?"

It's not what *I* want. In fact, the second I saw her down in the lobby, I wanted to toss her over my shoulder and spank her ass red for letting anyone else see her looking so very fuckable.

It's why I refused to renew our memberships to Black Light, where we played for free for the last month. I didn't like anyone else looking at her. It brought out a violence in me that I had to contain. Had to be careful not to channel into our play.

"I dressed for you, Master," she says softly.

Damn. Every time I try to defend myself against this relationship, she says something like that.

A surge of passion rushes out of me, and I grip her face in both my hands and shove her up against the wall again, kissing the hell out of her pretty mouth.

By the time I'm finished, my beard has chafed her skin, her lips are swollen, and she's panting for breath. I want to do a hundred dirty things with her, but I shove my dark desires down. The need to make up for hurting her feelings takes precedence over my need to torture that lush little body of hers.

I smooth back her hair. "If we don't leave this room now," I warn her, "you'll be naked in thirty seconds with my handprints all over that pretty ass of yours."

Her eyes dilate. "Mmm."

"I meant that as a threat." Amusement rolls around in my mouth, almost making me smile. "Let's go eat."

"Yes, Master."

I maneuver her out of the room with my hand on her back because it's so damn pleasurable to have her body under my hands at all times. In the elevator, I flatten her against the wall again. "Were you a good girl this week?"

She blinks up at me. "I'm always a good girl."

"I know." I brush the hair out of her face. "That's what makes this so wrong."

Her brows furrow in confusion. "What?"

"You're so good, and I'm very, very bad."

She doesn't balk. I don't think she believes me—but she should. Insead, her sweet body writhes against mine, seeking pleasure. The elevator stops, and two people get on, prompting me to turn around and tuck Kayla protectively into my side. We're safe here—there's no bratva cell or anyone our cell has a beef with in Los Angeles.

I take her to the nice restaurant in the hotel because I don't want to get too far from our room. Once we're settled and ordered our food, Kayla studies me.

"What do you do for your job, Pavel?"

"Anything the boss wants me to," I say. *And nothing I can tell you about.* When I realize she's waiting for more, I add, "My position is *brigadier*--a soldier. I don't rank high in our organization, but I am lucky enough to be in our *pakhan's* inner circle."

"Ravil is the boss—the *pakhan*?" she asks.

My brows shoot up at her knowing his name. I haven't shared much of anything about my life with Kayla. We usually keep our conversation and activities to the bedroom.

"Sasha told me," she says quickly. Sasha, our bratva fixer's new bride, studied theatre with Kayla at University of Southern California. They roomed together during college. I now live with the pain-in-the-ass bratva princess and the rest of our bratva cell.

"Yes. He's getting pissed about me being gone every weekend. He made a comment."

"If you had to cancel, it would be fine. I'd understand." She flushes. "I mean, of course, you know that. You're the dom."

I'm the kind of guy who takes whether something is being offered or not, but having Kayla repeatedly offer up her submission changes me. Makes me want to give a little more. Which is what makes this dangerous territory. I shouldn't let this thing deepen when I'm about to break it off. So I don't tell her the truth: that I'd rather stick a fork in my eye than cancel our weekend.

Our food comes—steak for me, salmon salad for Kayla, and we eat in silence until Kayla asks, "Do you kill people for Ravil?"

The words charge the air between us, creating an electric barrier.

My brows slam down as my pulse quickens. "Why would you ask that, Kayla?" My gaze travels to her throat, marking her frantic pulse. The worst possibilities run through my head—she's an informant. She's wearing a wire. That's why she's asking about Ravil and my job and who I've killed.

But no—Kayla's such an open book. She couldn't play me like that, could she?

Her lips part, but no further sound comes out.

I reach across the table and pick up her wrist, finding her pulse with my fingers. "Why do you ask?" I repeat, with a harder edge to my voice.

She swallows. "C-curiosity." Her pulse is quick because I scared her, but it doesn't grow faster when she answers.

I flip her wrist in my hand and brush my thumb across her pulse lightly to soothe away my harshness of a moment ago. "You really want the answer?"

Her pulse skitters beneath the pad of my thumb. I can tell by her wide eyes that she already knows the truth, and it frightens her, but she nods.

"Yes. I told you I was a killer when we met. It wasn't a figure of speech." My admission thuds onto the table between us like a heavy stone, crowding our plates and silverware, an ugly centerpiece no one wants to look at. "All of them deserved it, not that I believe that will save my soul." I meet her gaze steadily. I resolved myself to being an executioner right after I dropped the first body for the Russian army. I never looked back. There's a place in this world for men like me. We serve a purpose most aren't willing to fulfill. But that place isn't anywhere near Kayla Winstead. She's far too pure. She's not innocent, not weak, but she's whole and undamaged. A man like me doesn't belong in her bed or her life.

She still hasn't spoken. I release her wrist and sit back in case she's ready to throw her napkin on the table and run. I wouldn't stop her.

"I'm not a nice man. I told you that when we met."

Her lashes flicker over her eyes, like she's trying to keep them wide, to keep tears from spilling. "Do you remember what *I* told *you*?"

I remember. I remember everything about that night. The way it felt to break her. The way it felt to hold her in my arms, afterward, and put her back together. The unspeakable sexual power that gave me.

I clear my throat. "You said you trusted me."

She nods. "I still do."

"Blossom." It's a sigh. Or maybe a prayer. I should set her free—right now—but I can't bring myself to speak the words. I'm not ready to give her up. So instead, I say, "I promise I'll let you go the moment you want out."

She draws back, and I watch a shiver move through her.

"You're scared," I murmur, reaching for her fingers across the table and weaving mine through hers. "Are you scared of me?"

"No." She shakes her head.

"Good. You're safe with me, blossom. Always. You say the word, I back off. You know that, right?"

She has a safe word. I'm telling her it extends beyond our play. If—no, *when*—she says *red* to this relationship, it ends. Because I know that day will come.

3

Kayla

After dinner, I fish in my purse for my bottle of eye drops and shake it, but it's empty.

Pavel watches, his face impassive. "You okay?"

"My eyes are itchy from allergies. I need to pick up some more eye drops. Maybe I can run to the drug store tomorrow."

"I can go tonight," Pavel offers. "There's one on the corner. I'll take you back to the room and walk over."

"I can walk with you," I protest, then quickly tack on a "Master." It's funny how much of a gentleman he is when we're out of the bedroom.

"You want to walk over? In your heels?"

"Yes," I say. The truth is, I don't want to be separated from him. There's so much emotional distance between the two of us still, I can't stand any more physical. Especially when I only have him for a short weekend. I also don't mind the heels. I have a high pain threshold—which comes in handy being Pavel's slave.

"All right, blossom. Let's go." I hear the shrug in his

voice. The doorman holds the door open for us, and we walk out. I shiver at the night air, and Pavel curses softly in Russian. "You're cold."

"I'm fine." I step into his side, and he takes the hint, wrapping an arm around me and holding me close to his hip as we walk. He was right—there's a drugstore just three-quarters of a block away, the neon sign shining, casting a blue glow on the sidewalk in front.

We step in. It's busy with Friday night activity. People stopping in to pick up six-packs or snacks for wherever they're going next. I find the eyedrops, and we walk up to the counter.

And that's when everything goes sideways.

Pavel's paying for the eyedrops when the guy behind us jostles me forward. Ravil's face contorts in anger, and he starts to turn, then goes perfectly still.

The guy has a gun out. He points it jerkily between our heads at the clerk. "Give me all the money in the register." He sounds panicked. Out of breath. God, why is he crowding me forward against the counter? Wouldn't it have been better for him to wait until we'd paid and moved away?

I let out an involuntary wounded cow sort of sound—a soft lowing of fear. I think the sound scares the robber because he seizes me and pulls me against his doughy belly. His jacket smells of gasoline, and the zipper digs into my back. He wraps me into a headlock, still keeping the gun pointed at the clerk.

I choke on my gasp. Time slows as I take in the horrified expression on the clerk and the flash of danger in Pavel's eyes.

Pavel doesn't hesitate. He grabs the guy's gun arm with his right hand at the same time he throat-punches him with his left. The gun points toward the ceiling and goes off. Screams sound all around us.

I wrench free, skittering back as Pavel slams the barrel of the gun against the guy's temple. His head makes a horrible sound when it cracks against the floor, his limbs sprawled in every direction.

Pavel's movements were as smooth as a choreographed movie fight. This isn't his first rodeo by any means. Or even his fifth. He points the pistol at the guy's face with obvious expertise. "You don't fucking touch my girl." His accent is thick, voice full of menace.

Chills race up and down my spine because I have zero doubts now that Pavel told me the truth: he's a stone cold killer.

And then I review what he said. *You don't touch my girl.* He did that for me. If the guy hadn't touched me, would he still have acted?

The clerk behind the register mutters, "*Whoa,*" like he's impressed.

It was damn impressive. Pavel's moves couldn't have been better choreographed if he was in a staged movie fight.

"Call the cops," Pavel tells the clerk without looking away from the guy he's aiming at.

Before I can catch my breath, another pistol emerges, this time from a guy at the door.

They were a team. This one can't be more than eighteen or nineteen years old. Thick dark curls hang in his face, and his gun hand shakes so hard I'm afraid he'll accidentally shoot the whole place up. He points it at Pavel. "Drop the gun," he orders, like he's watched too much crime TV.

Pavel's not impressed. In a clean sweep, he shifts the aim of his gun to the guy at the door, putting his foot on the chest of the guy on the floor, who is starting to rouse. "*Put it down*," he minces.

"Y-you put it down," the teenager insists. "Or I'll shoot."

"You'll be dead before you pull the trigger," Pavel advises him evenly. "I never miss a shot." I believe him. The way he sights straight down his arm and his steady hold of the gun screams expert. Sureshot.

Killer.

"*Damn*," the clerk murmurs with obvious appreciation.

The thug's face sort of crumples in defeat.

"*Slowly* put the gun on the floor."

The guy obeys, bending his knees and placing the gun down at his feet.

"Walk over here. Lie down beside your friend." He points at his feet. His steady focus never leaves the guy's face, and the pistol never wavers. "Anyone else here? You got other partners? Someone in a car outside?"

"N-no." He shakes his head, his long bangs falling over one eye. He crouches at Pavel's feet then starts to sit.

"Face down." Pavel nudges the first guy with his foot. "You, too. Roll over." When they're both on their bellies, Pavel curses in Russian.

"Can you pick up that gun, blossom? Carefully?" His voice is much softer when he speaks to me. Like he's trying to soothe me with quiet tones—the same way he does during a scene.

I move faster than I thought I could in stilettos and shaking legs and snatch up the gun. I bring it to him because holding it doesn't feel safe to me.

Pavel takes the second gun and tucks it in the waistband of his pants then reaches for my hand. "Are you okay? Are you hurt?"

"Yeah. I mean, no—I'm okay."

Pavel delivers a hard kick to the one who'd held me. His normally impassive face has hardened into something frightening. "You're lucky you'll be dealing with the cops and not me," he growls. "*Nobody* touches my girl."

The flag flying in my chest for Pavel whips and flaps at that, rocking me with simultaneous glee and horror. I'm dizzy at the idea he did all this for me. To protect me or to exact retribution. But for the first time, I am also scared. Because he looks positively murderous right now. He warned me all along—telling me he wasn't a nice man. Asking if I was afraid. Promising to let me go.

What would he do to this man if the cops weren't coming? Torture him? Kill him? I don't think I want to know.

A crowd of frightened customers has started to gather at the perimeter of the scene now that Pavel has subdued the robbers.

"Did you call the police?" Pavel asks the clerk.

"I tripped the alarm right away," he says. The wail of sirens reaches us, as if on cue.

"Are you a cop?" the awed clerk asks.

"Nah." Pavel doesn't illuminate the guy any further. Two cop cars screech up to the curb, the lights on their cars flashing blue and red into the store.

Pavel crouches to place both guns on the floor then stands, holding both hands in the air. Again, not his first rodeo.

The police run to the door, guns drawn. "Get down on your knees," one of them shouts.

I'm not sure who he's talking to, but Pavel understands perfectly. He kneels, hands still carefully held in the air.

"It's not him!" the clerk protests loudly, maybe even more upset than I am. "It was them," he points at the guys on the ground.

"Yes, it was them," I raise my voice in indignation.

Pavel's not upset, though. He's been through this before. Knows what to do. His face still wears the hardened mask. He definitely looks like he's been on the wrong side of the law more than a few times.

"Nobody move," the cop advises.

~

Pavel

"So you're the hero." The police officer who finally uncuffs me says it with total sarcasm. He's run my ID. Sees my tats. Knows what I am.

"No." I turn to face him and adjust my sleeves.

I saw this shitstorm coming the moment I got involved, but I had no choice. Now our evening is ruined.

Possibly more than our evening. Maybe this was what needed to happen to slam some sense into Kayla. Make her see I'm not the guy she wants as her boyfriend.

I see the way she looks at me now... like I'm a monster.

I should embrace it. Instead, the need to soothe her has me itchy and raw. I've been on police lock-down for more than forty minutes now as they got everybody's story and figured out what was what, and I've had to watch my little flower leaning against the counter like her legs won't hold her up.

I still want to kill the *mudak* who grabbed her. It would be a long, slow, bloody death.

"Where'd you learn those skills?" the cop asks, even though he must already know. If not from my ID, then from the tattoos on my knuckles.

"Russian military," I say gruffly. It's partly true. They began my training.

"Uh huh."

I beckon to Kayla, only half-certain she'll come. Whether she's still my slave. "Am I free to go?"

"Yes." I barely hear his answer because the relief that rips through me when she practically flies across the floor and into my arms makes the room spin.

I kiss the top of her head and rub her back. "Let's go, blossom. Did you get your eyedrops?"

"My eye drops!" she exclaims and whips her head around to look toward the counter.

The clerk holds the bag up for her. He has mistakenly decided I'm the hero in this scenario.

I'm not. I'm the avenger. Only for Kayla.

We don't speak as we walk back to the Four Seasons. When we're in the elevator, Kayla peers up at me.

This is it. I brace myself for a serious question or comment. How many men have I killed? What other crimes have I committed? Because she's seen with her own eyes that I'm not the good guy.

"If that guy hadn't grabbed me, would you have still disarmed them?"

I have to tell her the truth because she needs to hear it. She needs to know what I am. I shake my head. "No, *malysh*."

She blinks those baby blues at me. *Gospodi*, those eyes!

I try to explain. "I knew what a cluster that would be. How long it would take—it ruined our night. If we could have just walked out of there without being a part of it, wouldn't you have preferred that?"

She hesitates a moment then nods. "Yes."

The elevator doors open, and she steps out. I stand there a moment, digesting her unexpected agreement. But then, she's always agreeable. And it nearly always shocks me.

She turns, waiting for me to come out. "What does *malysh* mean?"

"Baby." I step out and touch her cheek.

She doesn't pull away—a good sign.

There's something different about Kayla, for sure. A steel beneath her softness that isn't usually there. Half of me thinks we're galloping swiftly to our end, but I can't be sure.

Maybe she's still digesting what happened.

Despite my idea that this is the moment that could—should—end it all, and that I should welcome that outcome, my desire to fix this—to scoop her into my arms and hold her like we've just finished a particularly intense scene sizzles and pops beneath my skin.

"Pavel?" There's a little pop of her lips on the "P" that makes me think of how badly I want those lips open around my cock, and then my name comes out like a little puff of air. "Master?" she corrects.

"*Da*?" I loop an arm around behind her back and pull her up against my body.

Her lips tick up when I speak Russian, like she thinks it's hot or something. "Can you… can we…"

I cock my head. I'm good at reading people, but I have no idea where she's going. I can detect lies; I can't read minds. "Say it," I command in no more than a whisper.

She swallows like she's nervous to ask me.

"What do you need, *malysh*?"

"I want you to fuck me."

I don't wait. I tuck my forearm under her hips to boost her up and carry her, straddling my waist toward our hotel room. I'm still trying to decipher why she hesitated to ask. "Did you mean *just* fuck you?"

She nips my earlobe. "Please, Master."

I manage to extract and tap the keycard against the

handle then kick the door open. "How do you want to get fucked?"

"Hard. Rough. Underneath you."

I set her down and peel off her dress. She's flushed, her hair tousled.

The ugliness of the convenience store seeps away. Maybe the night's not so ruined.

"You want missionary sex."

She checks my face, and when she sees I'm teasing, gets flirty, "Yes, but with a very rough missionary."

"Hmm. I'm not sure those exist." I unbutton my shirt and toe off my shoes. "Lose the clothes. Missionaries definitely don't wear heels and thigh-highs to bed."

She scrambles to obey as I strip out of my clothes, too.

"Open the bed. We have to be under the sheets, right?"

"N-not necessarily."

I reach past her and yank down the bedcovers. "I'm just giving you a hard time. Get in bed, *printsessa.*" I follow her in and crawl over the top of her. "Close your eyes."

I wait until she's obeyed before I part her thighs and lower my head to lick into her. She's already wet and juicy. "What got you wet, blossom? Me fighting for you?"

"Yes," she admits.

I want to ask more, but she tastes too good to continue the interrogation. I roll my tongue around her clit, lick her sex like a juicy peach. I don't stay long enough to make her come—my cock aches to be inside her already —again.

Always.

I climb over her and slide in, groaning inwardly at how good it feels. "You need it rough, baby?"

She rocks her hips up to meet mine. "Yes, sir. *Yes.*"

I pull back and slam in hard, bracing one hand against the headboard. "This hard?" I thrust again, throwing out my free hand to catch her shoulder when I realize her head is going to hit the wood.

Her eyes roll back in her head. "*Yes.*"

Well, damn. Missionary never felt less vanilla. The same heady power courses through me as when we scene. Her moans mingle protest with desire as I hold her in place to drill her.

I move my hand from her shoulder to her throat. I've held her throat before but loosely, symbolically. Now I have to hang on to keep her from hitting her head. Her eyes fly open, alarm registering.

The sadist in me fucking loves her fear, and I slam in even harder. I know I won't hurt her, but she doesn't know how far I'll go.

She cries out, so I know she can safe word if she needs to. I'm not cutting off her air. Her cries grow frantic, needy. Her legs thrash beneath me.

All the adrenaline that pumped through my veins at the convenience store finds its release now—given a far more delicious purpose the moment Kayla made her request. I've never needed to fuck so hard. To violently pleasure myself and a partner.

Kayla sobs with desperate desire. "*Master.*" I don't know if she's begging to come or for me to stop, but the pleading word brings on the hardest orgasm of my fucking life.

I come and come and come inside her, forgetting to give her permission.

"May I—?" She's already coming, her tight channel squeezing my dick in quick pulses.

"Come." I keep rocking into her, slowing the force and speed of my thrusts but still nowhere near gentle. I keep my hand wrapped around her throat as I claim her pouty lips, kissing the hell out of her, my facial hair reddening her baby soft skin.

"Was that what you needed, blossom?" My voice sounds rough, as if I'd been the one shouting a release.

"Yes." She pants, a sheen of sweat making her tits look slick and inviting. I release her throat and trail my hand over one of them, thumbing her nipple.

I lower my body over hers, blanketing her as I nuzzle into her neck. "You're beautiful when you come without permission."

Her breath stalls for a moment, and then she gets defensive. "You said *yes*."

"Mm."

She wriggles beneath me, and I roll us to our sides, still connected. "I said yes to save you from punishment. Don't expect I'll always be so merciful."

The room is dark—I never turned on the lights—but I think I detect a blush.

I ease out of her and roll onto my back, the post-orgasm relaxation settling in swiftly.

"You're mean," she murmurs, nestling against my side and scraping the tip of her nail over my nipple.

I cover her hand and pull her fingers to my lips. "You like it." I close my eyes, listening to the hum of pleasure running through my body. Marveling at what Kayla does to me. How sex with her can flip a situation so completely. "Well, this went in a totally different direction than I expected," I tell her, uncharacteristically open with my thoughts.

She pauses a moment. "What did you expect?"

I make a non-committal sound, then I just admit it. "I was pretty sure you were going to call *red* on the whole thing."

She sits up, pulling the sheet up to cover her breasts like

she's feeling vulnerable. She stares straight ahead. "Do *you* want to end this?"

I roll to my side to see her face in the shadows. I can't, for the life of me, figure out why she sounds hurt.

I also can't explain the alarm that spreads through me. When we were walking back and I was assigning odds to the chance of her ending things, I was troubled but still calm as hell. Right now, adrenaline spikes through my system, and my skin prickles like I'm in physical danger. Or like she is.

She's asking me point blank. I could end things right now. Do what I planned to do. Before things get serious. Before I have to choose between the brotherhood and love. Between atoning for my sins in Russia and staying here with her.

I should say *yes*. Explain how this is a bad idea. Right now. There won't be a better time.

"No." I sound angry.

She finally looks at me. "Then stop suggesting it." Her voice is soft, but she's never sounded so firm. Like she's giving me an ultimatum that I hardly understand.

Stop suggesting it.

Fuck.

4

Kayla

After a morning of torturing my body in the best possible way, Pavel tries to book a spa appointment for me at the Four Seasons.

"I'm sorry, but we book weeks in advance, there's simply nothing available," I hear the spa attendant tell him over the hotel phone.

"That's okay, I'm good." I sidle up to him. "Feeling pretty relaxed already," I murmur.

He hangs up and loops an arm around me. "What should we do?"

I have this strong urge to get us out of the hotel room. I think that's why I wanted to walk with him to the convenience store last night. All of our interactions are in the bedroom or BDSM club, which is amazing. But I want more. Or I want to find out if there's the possibility for more.

I should be running for the hills after what I saw last night. Seeing what Pavel's capable of, being reminded that the world he lives in is far, far different from mine, should have been the clincher. It should have driven home the idea that I shouldn't pursue more from this guy. We are just sex, and I should be happy with that.

But my ambitious little heart won't take no for an answer. I have the need to be claimed fully by him. I'll never forget how spectacularly freeing it felt at Black Light when he scooped me up and told me I belonged to him now.

I want to belong to him. I like belonging to him.

And I know I do right now in the master-slave fantasy sense, but I want it in the real-life sense, too. Or, at least I think I do.

Maybe that's plain nuts.

"Why don't I show you L.A.?" I suggest then wince a little, already anticipating his rejection of the idea. In our relationship, I don't drive. He does.

But he blinks and shrugs. "Sure. I didn't rent a car this time, but we could ride share somewhere."

"I have my car. I mean, it's not fancy, but we could take it. You could drive, if you want," I add hastily.

The corners of his lips tick up. "Yeah, okay. I don't need fancy."

"No?" I move to my suitcase to grab something to wear—Pavel's kept me naked all morning, even after my shower.

Pavel makes a soft scoffing sound. "You must know I don't come from money, Kayla."

I put on my bra and a long-sleeved turquoise shirt that makes my boobs look great. "I actually don't know much about you at all, Master." I use the honorific *Master* to keep it from sounding like a complaint, which it really is.

He must hear it for what it is because as I start to put on my panties, he looks over and demands, "Why are you wearing panties?"

I pull them on anyway, feeling impish. "For protection. Because my master likes to spank me far too much." I giggle and sidle away from him when he advances.

"Sassy. I like it when you're naughty." I think I expect him to chase, but he takes his time following me, forcing me to stop and wait for him to arrive. His hands settle on my hips. "Take them off."

I lift my chin, a gleeful challenge in my eyes.

Pavel considers me. For the thousandth time, I wish he wasn't so darn hard to read. I can't even tell if he's amused by my antics or annoyed. "You want me to chase you and take them off, myself, don't you?"

I keep playing, slipping out of his grasp with a breathy laugh.

"I like it better when you obey."

I freeze. I was up for earning a little punishment, getting myself in trouble, but not for his dissatisfaction with me. "Sorry, Master." I move to take them back off.

Pavel follows me. "*Nyet*, that's not true. I like you sassy, too." He manacles my wrists and yanks me up against his chest.

My breath leaves me, and I look up at his harsh, handsome face, thrilled he's finally getting playful. He slowly twists my arms behind my back, turning me to face the bed. "Is this what you wanted, blossom?" he whispers in my ear. "To be forced?"

"Yes."

He pushes my torso down and smacks my bare ass. "I don't think I can do pretend non-consent."

"Okay."

He doesn't move, just holds me in the position, suspended in his refusal. "It's not that I don't like it, Kayla." It feels like an admission. A confession. Like I'm hearing something real, maybe for the first time. "I do."

He rubs away the sting the single spank left. "I just… Fuck. I like it way too much."

I'm trembling, and not from the scene, for once. Because of the rawness of his confession. Is this why he always holds back? He's afraid of his own dark desires?

"I trust you," I tell him.

He makes a dissenting sound in his throat.

"I have a safe word. I would use it if I wanted." I'm new to this world, but Pavel's been a perfect partner. He reads me. He's careful. He pays attention.

He strokes my ass, circling it. He's silent for what feels like forever, then he finally says, "You're too trusting."

For some reason, that offends me. I love submitting to Pavel, letting him run the show completely, making all the decisions for us. But this feels like he's criticizing my submission—the one thing I bring to this very limited relationship.

"Screw you," I snap.

Pavel proves my judgement is perfectly sound by immediately releasing my wrists and stepping back.

I straighten and whirl to face him, heat flushing my cheeks. His brows are down, confusion playing over his features.

"Don't question the one thing I bring to this… *arrangement.*" I can't even bring myself to call it a relationship.

He takes another step back and holds his hands up in surrender. "Wait—the *one* thing? Fuck that."

Fascination overtakes my anger at seeing irritation pierce Pavel's cool facade. I'd take any real emotion from him at this point.

He stoops to pick up my panties and hands them to me. I guess I now have permission to put them on. "Kayla…"—he shoves his hand through his hair—"You bring everything. You bring you. That's all I want."

I pull on the panties and a pair of skinny jeans, facing away from him for a minute. Unmoored, bobbing in unknown waters, I don't even know what I want.

"Hey." Pavel wraps an arm around my waist from behind and yanks me back against him. He fists my hair. "Tell me why you're mad."

I realize this is what I wanted all along. To be claimed. Captured. I don't want to be adrift on my own trying to navigate these choppy waters.

"You act like I'm making a mistake, and I shouldn't be with you. It's the same as you always dangling the end over my head. I don't like it."

He's silent for a beat, then says, "Complaint received and noted." He bites my ear. Not a nip, but a solid bite. A little punishment for my outburst. My panties get wet. He still holds me captive.

"I'm sorry, Master," I say, now that I've expressed myself. "Am I in trouble?"

"Definitely. Lots of trouble."

I'd be nervous, but I detect the purr in his voice. This is the messiest non-relationship relationship I've ever had. It feels like a tightrope walk with no net, but the exhilaration is addictive.

"I'll save it for tonight." He slides his hand between my legs, rubbing the seam of my jeans up against my clit. Now my panties are completely soaked. "Right now, I'm expecting an L.A. experience."

Pavel

The first thing I think when I climb behind the wheel of Kayla's ten-year-old Camry is that I want to buy her a new car. It's obscene how much I want to shower this girl in gifts, which is why we're at the Four Seasons Beverly Hills instead of somewhere even a little more reasonable.

I live a lavish lifestyle right now, but it's on the *pakhan's* dime. Getting sent to America to work for Ravil while I was lying low was the best thing that ever happened to me. Ravil brought benevolence, reason and stability when all I'd ever known before was violence and chaos. He takes good care of his cell. We live in style. I have no living expenses, which means all my earnings go straight into savings. Savings I plan to use to set myself up back in Russia when things cool off there. Another reason I should've broken things off with Kayla last night.

After fussing with the radio, she sits on her hands beside me, stealing sidelong glances.

"What are you thinking?" I demand. That's one of the insane benefits of being a dom. I can make her talk but don't have to offer a thing myself. It's cruel and wrong, I know, but suits me to a fucking tee.

Her gaze zips back to the windshield. "Nothing. Just checking."

I don't know if I let the smile show, but it's definitely there, in my chest. My crazy little slave is always checking in with me—making sure she's pleased me. "We're good," I tell her, in case she's still worrying about our fight back in the hotel room.

I know she wants more from me. She expects me to open up and share something. Maybe not the way she bares her soul to me, but crumbs, at least. It's just not my way. Never has been.

But as I follow her directions out to the highway, I sense her nervous energy growing more frenetic. She's a tempest in a teapot, this one. A mercurial ball of energy, fascinating to watch, easy to direct. But also shockingly combustible when I fuck up and miss giving her what she needs.

"Where are we going?"

She shoots another glance at me, like she's trying to figure out if she got it right. "Venice Beach. Is that okay? I don't know if you're a beach person—"

"It's good," I cut her off. "I want to see what you like here."

"I'm not a beach person, I mean, I don't go swim or lay out in the sun, but I like to walk down the pier. It's where I go to think."

My phone rings as I'm driving, and I pull it out of my pocket. "I'm sorry, I've got to take this," I tell Kayla and put it on speaker since her car doesn't have a hand-free option.

My mom's lonely voice fills the car. "Pavel?"

"*Da, Mama,*" I answer her in Russian. "Is everything okay?"

"Yes. I just… hadn't heard from you for a while."

Guilt rips through my chest—not just for not calling more, but for not being there. Especially after what I did.

"Sorry, Mama. I'm in Los Angeles. It's a city in California—with a beach," I add because my mom knows nothing about America.

"Oh?" She sounds so lost, but it's nothing new. She's been lost my entire life. Trauma and abuse have made her vacant and withdrawn. Barely functioning in reality. And she was my good parent. It's no fucking wonder I'm an emotionless *mudak.*

"I—" I look over at Kayla, who's listening raptly, despite the fact that she doesn't speak Russian. "I'm with a woman." I don't know why I'm telling my mom that. I'm making this thing with Kayla way more important than it should be.

"Oh." My mom's surprised syllable has a hopeful tint to it. "That's nice. I'm sure you're very good to her."

My skin instantly crawls, heart dives into my stomach. A wave of oily sickness washes over me. Images of my mother cowering against a wall, my hands covered in blood, flash in front of my eyes. Me trying to protect her as just a young boy. She thinks I'm a hero.

Am I good to Kayla? Pretty fucking far from it.

I'm only a shade different from my father. Or maybe I'm not different at all, it's just Kayla who's different. A woman who likes to be hurt. Who gets excited by the pain I deliver, who likes to be kept on her knees, servile and sweet.

I change lanes on the highway, driving too fast. "I should go, Mama, I'm driving. I'll call you when I get back to Chicago, all right?"

"Yes, of course, Pavel. Be safe."

The sludge in my stomach twists. "Same. Bye." I end the call and grip the steering wheel too hard.

"Was that your mom?" Kayla asks.

"*Da*." I answer in Russian because I was just speaking it, then I remember to switch. "Yes."

"Is she all right?" Somehow Kayla got the essence of my mother, despite the language barrier.

"No. My mother is…" I trail off, not really wanting to have this conversation, but Kayla waits, those attentive eyes trained on the side of my face. "She's alone. I pay her bills. She's depressed, I guess. I had to leave her to come here, but I'm planning to go back."

There. I said it. Did I say it to drive a wedge between us? To inflict more cruelty, as is my way? Or am I just being honest for once? I sure as fuck don't know.

Kayla goes still. "When?"

I swallow. "I don't know. It depends on a lot of things."

Kayla is *not* one of those things. Or she shouldn't be. Why does it suddenly feel like she is?

"What things?" she presses, her voice so quiet I barely hear it over the radio.

"My *pakhan* and the state of a murder case back in Moscow. And money, I guess. I've been saving to get myself set up there when I go back."

I don't say she's part of the decision because she's not, yet I sense her drawing back and register her hurt.

"I should have told you that sooner, I guess. I'm sorry." I've owed her that apology for hours now—it feels like a relief to get it out.

"Well, how soon?" I hear a tinge of panic in her voice. "When do you think you'll move?"

I shake my head. "Could be months; could be years. I've already been here for three."

"Three years?"

"*Da*."

"Because of the murder case?" she whispers.

A tight band cinches around my throat to choke me. "Don't ask about that, Kayla," I manage to say around it. My throat is scratchy and raw.

She looks away from me, probably fighting back tears. *Blyad'*.

I approach Venice Beach and luck into a parking spot near the pier. I get out and walk around to Kayla's side to close her door after she climbs out. "Hey." I press her ass up against the car door, pinning her with my body. "I'm not going to offer you an out again because you told me not to, but I want you to know…I will always respect your wishes." In this one way, I can resist my genetic coding. I won't ever keep a woman prisoner until death do us part.

I see a mixture of fear and revulsion on her face, but it's warring with that misplaced faith she has in me, and I know the moment the faith wins out. She sort of firms up, the way she did last night after the convenience store. Like she's somehow reconciled herself to what I am and decided she still has backbone enough to stick around.

Crazy, beautiful flower.

"I know." She lifts her face like she wants to be kissed.

I mean to brush a kiss over her lips, but instead I find myself devouring her mouth with the most ruthless kiss ever taken. My cock thickens against her belly, and the desire to do all manner of terrible things to her over and over again for the rest of our lives makes me want to carry her away to some dark dungeon where I can chain her to my bed and feast on her delicate body.

I force myself back because it's broad daylight, and there are people everywhere. Not that Kayla seems to mind. It seems she'd follow my lead regardless of how insane I am. And that's one of the best reasons not to leave the status of this relationship up to her. For me to man up and end it before I hurt her.

But I don't fucking want to.

And I'm a stubborn asshole who usually gets what he wants.

I take her hand, adjusting my cock in my pants. "Show me this pier." My voice is gruff, deepened with desire.

"Yes, Master." She shoots a worshipful gaze my way that nearly drops me to my knees. I don't know how I got so fucking lucky, how I earned her trust when I've been nothing but a dick here, but I'm going to make sure I give her everything she needs while I still have her.

She deserves that much.

The pier is crowded with people, but we ignore them and walk out to the very end of it to lean on the rail. The ocean sparkles cobalt blue and frothy white—bright and hopeful, like Kayla.

"I came here my first weekend in Los Angeles. I moved out here to go to USC—that's where I met Sasha—and I was so excited to see the ocean. I drove out here by myself and watched the sunset. And that's when I promised myself I'd never give up on my dream."

"To become an actress?" I ask. I shift, so I'm standing behind her, protecting her back from the other people around. Or maybe just staking my claim. I wrap one arm around her waist and rest the other on the rail beside hers.

"Yes." She darts a glance my way. "Sometimes I think I should put a time limit on it. Like, I have one more year, and if nothing happens, I'll move back home. But then I remember the promise my eighteen-year-old self made, and I say never. I'm not leaving until I've made it where I wanted to go."

"And where is that?"

She drops her head a little, so I kiss her temple.

"Tell me. A-lister? Hollywood star?"

"Yes."

"You'll make it," I tell her, not because I know anything about show business but because I want it to be true. I want Kayla to have everything she always dreamed of. A woman as good and pure as her deserves to have the world at her feet. Mostly because it would surprise her. And she'd work her ass off to do it right.

"Sometimes I believe it, sometimes I don't," she whispers.

"Believe it."

She turns in my arms and looks up at me. "So I guess I should've told you that last night, too. I can't leave L.A. Not even for—" she breaks off. I think she was going to say *love* but lobbed that word off at the neck.

"So we'll enjoy what we have, no? While we have it."

She melts a little against me, like some raging conflict

has just been resolved. "I'm sorry if it seems like I am pushing for more. I don't—"

I put a finger on her lips. "No apology needed." Gently, I turn her back around, so we can stare at the sea together. The waves crash beneath us in a frothy foam. Someone's out with a boogie board, trying to catch a wave.

I should be glad. We just put an ending on our relationship. Not a specific date but an agreement that we'll part ways sometime in the future.

It's what I wanted. What needed to happen. Why, then, do I want to find some piece of wood and beat it until my knuckles bleed?

5

Pavel

When we return from the pier, I'm ready to play. "I want you naked, on the bed, now," I command, unbuttoning my cuffs.

Kayla's glassy, unfocused gaze instantly sharpens at my tone, and she scrambles to comply. She strips off all her clothes.

"I want you in the hose and heels," I say gruffly, my dick already hard again remembering how hot she looked last night in them.

I don't undress because that's how we roll—her naked; me clothed, for as long as possible. It helps set the power dynamic. She's my slave. Undressed for my eyes. Naked in every way to me. Right down to the soft marshmallow of her soul.

She crawls up on the bed in her black thigh-highs and stilettos and kneels in the center of it, hands face up on her thighs, awaiting instruction. I let my gaze roam over the beautiful picture she makes. The pose. Her tight little body. Her youthful tits with the pale peach nipples that stiffen at my slightest touch. I memorize it all for when I'm away from her. I'll fuck my fist all week remembering all the beautiful ways she submitted to me during our time together.

"Good girl," I praise, strolling close and tweaking one of her pouty nipples now. "I should have asked if you need to eat first. Are you hungry?"

She hesitates then shakes her head.

"Words, blossom."

"No, sir."

"All right. We'll play. Then I will feed you."

I will feed you. Simple words, but saying them affects me. Like she's my pet, and I decide if and when she gets fed. The control she gives to me—putting me in charge of her body, her wellbeing—is a powerful drug.

I torture secrets out of men for a living, but I didn't know I was a sadist until last year.

No, that's a lie. I always knew I had this thing inside me. It's why I had a mountain of rules about never laying a hand on a woman. None of my bratva brothers—at least none of the ones in my current cell—can stomach hurting a woman. But me? My deepest, darkest fear was that I *could* stomach it. That I might like it. Far too much.

And I discovered I do.

To make it worse—or perhaps to make it work—I'm not sure which—I somehow landed the sweetest, most submissive, angel of a slave. Which means I must be constantly vigilant for signs I've gone too far.

I open my suitcase to unpack my toys. Nipple clamps to begin with and a buttplug. I often like to start by claiming her most vulnerable parts while I play with the rest.

I bought her new nipple clamps—beautiful flowers that will cover her areolas with tiny bolts that tighten against her nips.

As I approach, Kayla's stomach audibly growls. I stop and arch a brow, hiding my amusement. "Uh oh. Did you just lie about being hungry?"

She flushes, guilt scrawling over her expressive face. Her big blue eyes plead with me. She knows I'll punish her transgression.

"Lying is a serious offence, blossom."

Her big eyes get even bigger and her mouth goes slack. She doesn't answer. I put a knuckle under her chin. "Tell me, beautiful. Did you lie because you didn't want to disappoint me?"

She doesn't answer. Her deer-in-the-headlights look will go in my spank-bank for the week. "Or did you lie because you wanted to play before you ate?" When she still doesn't answer, I guess again, "Or was it a combination of the two?"

She nods and licks her lips, which makes my dick go rock hard. "A combination of the two. —Sir," she adds hastily.

She's so fucking adorable. Like, makes-my-chest-squeeze adorable.

"All right, here's what we're going to do." I walk to the dresser to find a room service menu. "I'm going to order us some dinner, and then I'm going to punish you for lying. Hopefully I'll be through by the time the food gets here." I bring the menu over, sitting beside her on the bed to share the view. "What sounds good?"

She quickly scans the menu. "I'll take the Caesar salad, Master."

"With chicken?"

"Yes, please. Master."

I brush my lips over her bare shoulder because it looks so delectable and leave to call in our food. "Tell them to knock when they get here and then leave it outside the room," I instruct. No fucking way I'd open the door with a chance of anyone seeing Kayla like this, even if she was under the covers or in the bathroom. I want her to feel vulnerable with me—not to the outside world. Plus, I'd have to kill anyone who saw her naked.

Not a joke.

I return to my suitcase full of toys and unpack a few more surprises then return. "Come off the bed for a minute." I beckon to her, and she crawls toward me. I hold her elbow as she swivels her legs around to stand on her sexy heels. I sit on the bed and hold her between my legs. Her glorious tits are in my face, nipples pouting, begging to be tortured. I take one in my mouth and suck it to an even stiffer peak.

Kayla moans softly.

Sweet little slave.

I slide the flower plate over her nipple and tighten the screws, watching her face closely to judge when it's enough. When she sucks in her breath and shifts on her two feet, I give her a second to see if she acclimates or whether I need to back off. She seems to, so I leave it and move onto the next nipple, first sucking it, rolling it around over my tongue, then fastening the plate over the top and tightening the clamps.

She whimpers a little, her belly shuddering in on a breath. I stroke my hands up and down her sides.

"Over my knee, blossom," I intone quietly. I'm the type of dom who generally keeps his commands soft. The more trouble she's in, the quieter I get. It keeps her straining to listen, to hear me, to please me.

She dives over my lap like a good girl. I take another mental picture because the sight is so fucking beautiful. The thigh-highs have tiny bows at the tops and a thick black seam that runs down the centers of her legs before it plummets into the high heels. They frame her bare ass perfectly. She shifts and squirms a little, arranging her breasts underneath her on the bed. I love the curve of her long slender back as it slopes down from my lap to the mattress.

I take my time, using the flat of my hand to warm her ass up. I relish the sting on my own palm as I deliver pain to her, which isn't like me. I'm usually the guy who refrains from exerting himself too much in an interrogation. I stand back and watch Oleg, our enforcer, deliver the pain. Even with my first BDSM partners, I preferred distance from their bodies and the use of an implement. I'd bend them over a chair and use a long cane—maximum pain at minimal effort on my part.

But with Kayla, everything's different.

In one of our late-night virtual sex sessions last week, she confessed she prefers to be over my lap. She likes to be close to me, even when I'm inflicting pain. That's what this woman is all about.

She's not a pain slut. She's a pleaser. A service submissive.

Not what I thought I wanted, but now that she's mine, I would never wish for anything different.

I stop when she starts to squeeze her ass and wiggle like it's too much, then I stroke between her legs. She's sopping wet, her folds swollen, her cunt open like a flower for me. I pry her ass cheeks apart and drop a dollop of lube onto her anus, loving the involuntary squeeze of muscles when it hits. I take a stainless steel buttplug and start working the tip into her ass.

"Don't ever lie to tell me what you think I want to hear you say," I tell her. "I can't make good decisions as your dom when you do. I'm not good at reading your mind."

"I disagree, sir," she says softly. "Respectfully."

Unbearably cute.

Her anus opens, and I slowly push the plug forward. She mewls when it gets to the widest part.

"Deep breath," I advise. When she exhales, I push forward again, seating the plug. "Well, I don't know you inside out, yet. We're still learning each other, aren't we?" I pump the plug gently.

"Yes, sir." Her voice is shaky.

"You have to give me the facts, so I can make good decisions. If you're not sure, you could just say *I'm hungry, but I'd like to play first.*"

"I'm sorry," she says.

"Mmm. I like you sorry," I admit and resume spanking her, harder this time. The smacks on her ass jostle the plug, and she's quickly gasping and moaning from the mixture of pain and pleasure.

When I've turned her ass a gorgeous shade of pink, I lift her to stand between my knees again.

Her eyes glisten with tears. Seeing them always delivers a powerful punch. My dick gets harder than stone, and at the same time, I need to comfort her. The fact that she accepts comfort from me never fails to leave me changed. Almost as cracked open as I leave her.

I cup her hot ass, massaging it roughly as I lean forward and kiss her flat belly. "Are those tears because I hurt you, or are you sad you're being punished?"

She swallows. "Punished," she murmurs, like she can only get the one word out.

I stroke my palm down her outer thigh. "I know, you're a pleaser, blossom. You don't like to get it wrong, do you?"

She shakes her head, looking even more distraught.

Something twists in my chest.

"Come here, little flower." I pull her toward me, helping her to straddle my knees. She seems to like the closeness, leaning in to nuzzle my neck, putting those glorious tits in my face. I kiss the side of one and fiddle with the plug in her ass, rotating it, slowly pumping it.

Her breath rate increases, and she starts to moan softly at the stimulation. Soon she's humping my lap, rubbing that wet cunt over the bulge of my erection.

Fuck. I've already had her once, but I'm ready to go again. I unzip my pants and pull my dick out again. I sink into her heat for a second time.

"I'll let you in on a little secret, blossom." I pull her over my cock in a slow undulation.

She pulls back to meet my gaze, to show me she's listening.

"You can't get it wrong with me."

She blinks. The tears are long gone, replaced by a glassy sheen over her huge, blown pupils.

"Punishing you gives me pleasure, so I'm never disappointed. I don't need you to obey me every time or to read my mind or get it right. I just need your surrender, which you give so beautifully."

Her expression relaxes.

I slide backward on the bed and lie back, carrying her with me. "Ride me, blossom. Show me how you get yourself off."

She braces her hands on my shoulders and arches her back, giving me a glorious view from below.

Snap: Mental picture #3.

Actually, this time it's a mental video clip. Of Kayla working herself into a frenzy over my dick. Of the sounds she makes, keening and desperate. Of the curve of her throat, the bounce of her tits. I release her nipples from the clamps, trying to time the pain she'll experience when the blood rushes back to them with her orgasm. It works. After a few seconds, she slows her hips. She holds her breasts and cries out, her back bowing, head falling back. She stops completely as her muscles spasm and tighten around my dick.

I don't come. I'm too caught up in capturing every nuance of Kayla's orgasm for my mental movie. There's nothing more beautiful in the entire universe than watching her orgasm. I will go to my grave with the image of every single orgasm I gave her memorized. She exhibits total abandon, giving herself over completely to the pleasure. Sometimes she can't speak for long moments afterward, like her mind went so far it takes effort to bring it back.

"Beautiful, blossom." I pull her off me and flip her on her belly. Her ass is still pink from the spanking I gave her and seeing my handprints gives me a surge of pleasure. I straddle her thighs and enter from behind, wrapping my hand loosely around the front of her throat.

I don't need long. Watching her come is the most powerful aphrodisiac there is. I'm ready to go off the moment I'm inside her. I tug her throat, making her arch her back or get choked.

She lets out a cry—there's a little protest in the note but also a stark need, like she could come again in a heartbeat.

"Come again without permission, and I'll use my belt," I warn her.

"Please!" she gasps, sounding frantic.

I'm desperate, too. I don't answer, more because I'm so close to orgasm myself than because I want to make her suffer.

"Please. *Master*."

"*Come*." I force the word out as my balls draw up tight. I'm surprised to hear a gutteral sound come out of my mouth—it's not like me to reveal too much. But that's what this woman does to me.

I can't help it. The release is too great. I slam home and fill her channel with the small amount of cum that's regenerated since the last time I fucked her. It's a hundred times more pleasurable than the first time, but there's no taking mental pictures or standing back to observe because I'm as far gone as she is, letting her sweet pussy squeeze every last drop of cum out of me as she milks me for more.

As my consciousness seeps back into my body, I flinch when I realize my hold on her throat might be too tight. I instantly relax my fingers. I will punch my own face if I bruised her neck.

Could she even breathe?

Yes. Yes, I remember she was begging to come. She cried out with me. Panted with me. I lower her torso to the bed, following. I kiss between her shoulder blades, shift her pale hair away from her nape to brush my lips along the side of her neck.

"You okay?" I ask between the tiny kisses I shower along her jaw.

"Yes. Yes, sir," she remembers to add. She's not so far gone this time.

I pull out and roll her to her back, so I can inspect her throat, fighting back the sick feeling in my stomach at what I could've done. I run my finger across the faint marks. "Did I scare you?"

That's the last thing I want with Kayla. Nervous, sure. Eager to please. But never scared. Everything hinges on her trust.

That she gives it so blindly, so easily, often makes me want to smash things. I don't deserve the trust she puts in me, and I use it to hurt her.

But she likes it. That's what I remind myself on a daily

basis, every time I'm ready to walk away from this madness.

Her eyes are unfocused, but she finds my face, shaking her head. "No, Master." As if she senses my inner dilemma, she assures me, "I loved it."

Fuck.

This beautiful little flower.

6

Kayla

I'm still shaking when Pavel wraps me up in the soft blanket he brought and produces our dinner. I never heard the knock, but then, I was a little busy.

He left the plug in my ass, leaving me still enervated and horny, despite my—how many times did I orgasm? I can't even think.

Pavel places the tray beside me, uncovers my plate, and sets it on my lap, somehow knowing that my fingers aren't steady enough to pick it up yet. He leaves his own plate untouched, moving the tray away to sit beside me, drawing me against his side.

I lean into him, needing his strength to steady my wobble. This is the most terrifying part of every scene. It's not the nerves leading up to it—although those kill me. It's not the surrender—that part's easy for me. It's not the pain, when there's pain. And humiliation doesn't bother me.

It's the vulnerability when it's over. The sense of having been cracked open and poured out, like a raw egg in the mixing bowl. That's when the separation of our bodies—the distance between us, no matter how small—feels too great.

The night Pavel won me at the roulette wheel, I totally lost it when he pulled away.

He knows better now.

He stays close. Holds me until I stop clinging. And this is when I get the real Pavel. At least, I've decided this is the real Pavel. He doesn't show his cards often—his expression is usually dark and brooding or inscrutible and blank. He can be a dick. Honestly, I think that's his natural state. But after he's bared me, pulled me apart, shattered my defenses, after we've both come, when I'm in danger of crashing hard, that's when he turns tender. Grateful. Terribly protective.

In my darker, more jaded moments, I fear it's not because he cares, it's just because he wants more. He does what he's learned he has to do to keep me, no more, no less. He's a sadist, he needs a slave. This isn't a relationship—it's an arrangement.

He unwraps my silverware from the linen napkin and stabs a piece of chicken on my salad with the fork, then holds it to my mouth. I accept the bite, hungrier than I knew. He continues to feed me until my plate is empty, and only then does he reach for his plate of food—a club sandwich which he polishes off in no time.

I steal a glance at the hard planes of his face. He notes it, impassive as ever.

It's the same way he punishes me. Always even-tempered. Cool. He's quite suave and manicured for a man who's covered in crude tattoos that I think must represent heinous crimes.

"You don't get mad do you?" I dare ask him. He's not

talkative by nature. I have to push and pry to get anything out of him.

"Rarely." He slides his dark gaze to mine. Sometimes I catch a tortured look on him after we play. Like he's afraid of what he's done.

The truth is, I'm always a little scared of him—that's half the excitement. But I'd never run. I need this as much as he does. I crave the emotional tumult of being broken apart and put back together over and over again by him.

He picks my plate up off my lap, stacks it on his and sets them both back on the tray. "First of all, blossom, if I ever was actually mad, I wouldn't touch a hair on your head. That's a promise."

I was right. He's making sure I know I'm safe.

"I know you wouldn't hurt me." I don't know why I'm so sure, but I am. He's too conscientious a dom for me to believe he'd ever harm me in anger.

"I am dangerous, Kayla." He shoots me a look that seems to convey a warning of some kind. That I'm too generous in my opinion of him. "But it won't be an issue. I don't get mad."

"You get even?" I quirk a smile.

His lips twitch. "Precisely. I'm not the type of guy who runs hot. Except when my dick is in your mouth." He gives me one of his rare bad-boy grins. It makes him look at least five years younger.

My heart flutters at the sight.

~

Pavel

"I guess I'd better take you downstairs for a drink. You're too beautiful to be hidden away although I'll throat punch anyone who tries to talk to you."

Kayla's laugh is nervous, like she's not sure if I'm joking.

I'm not.

I'm a jealous, possessive motherfucker. Strange for a guy who's never had a girlfriend in his life.

But ever since the moment I broke her at Black Light, when Maxim, my bratva brother told me I own her now, I've been possessive as hell.

It's irrational because the possibility of this working out longer than another five minutes is slim.

Kayla climbs off the bed and pulls on another sexy dress—a red one this time. "No panties," I tell her when she starts to pull them on. She steps back out of them and smooths the skirt of her dress.

"Come on, beautiful."

"Master." She turns those big blue eyes on me. They're pleading. My dick turns as hard as marble despite the fact that I've already come twice. That's what this girl does to me.

Calling me *Master.*

Letting me call all the shots.

"Hmm?" I raise my brows in an authoritative way, making her blush and grow more nervous.

"May I take the buttplug out?"

I didn't forget. I wondered how much she could take. Whether she'd complain. I like to keep her ass prepared for anal sex. I like to keep her ass plugged in general, just to edge her.

"Are you getting sore, blossom?"

She nods her head.

"Come here." I sit on the edge of the bed again and hold my hand out to her. She steps between my knees, and once more, I fold her over my lap in her favorite position. She doesn't like impersonal torture. Or much distance between us. As a man who's kept everyone at arm's length for all of my life, it should be a difficult adjustment. But with Kayla, it's not. If she wants something, she gets it. Because she gives me *everything.*

The red of her earlier spanking is fading, so I spank her some more, loving the way she wriggles and pants and whimpers.

I grip the hand of the plug and gently pull it out, then push it back in. "Who does this hole belong to, little slave?"

Kayla gasps in surprise. "Y-you, Master," she warbles. I work it some more, fucking her ass with it until she's humping my lap. "Master, please," she begs.

"Please what, blossom?"

"Please…" She sounds so pitiful. I should have mercy on her, but instead it just makes me crave more of her begging. "I have to...I'm going to…"

"Permission to come," I tell her quickly because she's about to climax anyway, and I don't want to punish her more. I mean, of course I do, but not at this precise moment.

She climaxes as I give the plug short, quick thrusts in and out of her ass. She sobs out her release, and I spank her some more for good measure. "I wanted you sitting on this plug in that cocktail bar, remembering who owns you." I alternate slapping each cheek, not holding back much in the intensity. "But since you need me to take it out, I'll have to make your ass red and hot instead."

"Ohhh," she moans, still humping my lap. I stop spanking and roughly massage her ass. Pulling out the plug takes coaxing because she tightened around it when she orgasmed, but I manage to ease it out.

"Stand up, beautiful."

She wobbles when she gets up, still wearing her sexy

stilettos. I steady her with a hand on her elbow then wash and sterilize the plug for later.

Kayla's flushed and off-balanced, just the way I like her. When I return from the bathroom, I wrap an arm around her from behind and kiss her temple. "Good girl," I murmur because I know how much those words mean to her.

She lets out a whimper-sigh, relaxing back against me. She's so precious. I wish I could keep her.

I kiss her again. "Come on, little flower." I take her hand and lead her to the elevator.

Downstairs, the cocktail lounge is full and hopping. The young, good-looking and rich of Beverly Hills all gather here to drink and talk loudly. There aren't any tables, but I score one barstool at the bar, which I help Kayla onto. She fusses with her dress to keep from flashing her bare beaver as she gets up. Not that she has a beaver. She's freshly waxed—another gift for me. I get to mark her smooth, soft skin with rug-burn from my facial hair.

I squeeze my body in beside her, my hand on her back, making it clear she's with me.

Kayla doesn't know what she wants. I could order for her, and she'd drink whatever I buy, but I'd rather find out what she likes. I ask for the cocktail menu and let her scan it. "What are you getting?" she asks.

I'm amused that she wants to know. She's always measuring me to figure out what I want from her. Maybe not now, for the drink, but these things matter to her. "Vodka, rocks. I'm boring. What looks good to you?"

"Maybe the Moscow mule." She points at the cocktail description.

Sweet girl. My lips tug up in the ghost of a smirk. "Russian drink. Good choice."

She flushes a little and shifts on the stool, reminding me

she's sitting on a bare, red ass. I take another mental snapshot. Some day Kayla will be famous, and I'll get to jack off to these memories thinking, *I knew her when.*

I hate that thought. Not the one of her being famous but of us being a distant memory.

I order the drinks. Hers comes in a copper mug, decorated with an orchid and garnished with blackberries. She takes a sip and closes her eyes. "Mmm. I love it." She's so damn cute.

I sip my drink in silence. It takes me a minute to realize the lack of conversation has grown awkward. Kayla's toying with her straw too vigorously, shooting glances around the room.

Blyad.'

I'm not used to making small talk. Sure, I call her when we're apart. When I'm back in Chicago and she's here, but those conversations are sex-driven. Me ordering her to masturbate, so I can watch or to tell me all her darkest desires. I don't ask about her work or about her day.

I wouldn't even know how to have a conversation like that.

Kayla swivels in her seat and scans the crowd, then tips her pretty face up to me. "Do you think it looks like I'm your whore?"

My brows slam down. "What?"

She sucks on her lower lip.

Fuck. These are the moments that shock me. When I find out the alarming thoughts going in her pretty head. Things I never would have considered. Like how I hurt her feelings when I checked in before greeting her.

"No," I growl. "I think you look like my very hot date. Why would you say that?"

She doesn't answer. There's a little furrow between her

perfectly waxed brows that I want to rub away. "What am I to you?"

Gah. I rub my forehead, my stomach sinking. This is where I cut her loose, and we crash and burn. I should tell her she means nothing to me. That I was her master, and she was my slave, and I can't keep flying out to L.A. every weekend. We need to become something else. I already told her the moment she's over it, it ends.

Except that's stupid because Kayla's not the kind to end things.

It's going to have to be me.

Say it. Now, before we get any deeper with this. Before I learn how to make small talk and ask about her day. Before she learns to depend on me.

Because I'm not that guy.

But those guileless blue eyes train on me. She's not accusing me of being less than what she wants—that's not her style, but there's a pleading in her gaze.

Am I really ready to give that up? Those pleading looks that make my dick hard? Her steady submission. The soft, breathy intones of *please, Master*? Am I willing to walk away from the perfect situation?

Fuck, no.

Not yet.

And that makes me an even bigger asshole.

I lift my shoulders in a casual shrug. "Lovers. Play partners. Dominant and submissive." I can only hope it's enough. That we can keep this arrangement going a little while longer. Another week. Maybe a month. I'm not ready to give her up, even though I should. Even though she's taking all my focus from the job. Even though I'm using my savings to spend big when I come here—money I planned to use as start-up capital when I go back to Russia.

Even though I'm losing face with the boss for being absent so much.

She looks away.

I catch her chin and turn her face to mine. "*Not* my whore. Definitely not that."

I'm alarmed when a sheen of tears coats her babydoll eyes.

"What do you want me to say—that I'm your boyfriend? Kayla, I'm not that guy. I'm so far from that guy. I...wouldn't know how to do the role justice."

She nods, her throat moving as she tries to swallow. She reaches for her drink and puts the straw to her lips, sucking it down until it slurps.

Fuck. I haven't felt this adrift since I went too far, bloodying my hands without orders, and got sent to America. I haven't *felt* this much, period.

"Is that what you wanted me to say?"

She drops her gaze to her empty drink. I signal to the bartender and point at it to get her another, then lean my forehead down to hers and wrap my fingers in her hair. "Don't lie," I whisper.

She stops breathing.

I pull back a little to see her face. Her eyes glisten again with tears.

As much as I love seeing her cry when we play, the tears destroy me when we aren't. They simultaneously make me want to run away very fast and kill someone. I never learned how to comfort a woman—I've had to learn it all on the fly with Kayla.

"Kayla, I'm not saying no."

Christ, what am I saying? Did those words just come out of my mouth? I was going to break things off with her this weekend not step it up. I catch her face with my chin and turn it back to me. "I just think I'd suck at it." I shrug. "But I'll try. If that's what you want."

Gospodi, am I nuts?

She turns those blue headlights on me. They're shining now, still bright with tears, but high beams are all for me. This girl destroys me with just her eyes. Every time.

I stroke her cheek softly with my thumb as I lower my lips to hers. I give her a soft, exploratory kiss. It's a promise, like a handshake to seal the deal. I'm her boyfriend now.

Fuck. I really have no idea what I'm doing. And no business making such a promise.

But when I pull away, her expression steals my breath. "You're happy now."

She nods.

Despite a thousand misgivings, my lips turn up, fascinated by the change in her. I can practically feel her joy in my own being, even though it's not an emotion I'm prone to experiencing.

Ever.

Jesus, how can I possibly make this work? Short answer —I can't. But somehow, I still have to try.

"You'll have to be very, very honest with me." I brush my thumb across her lower lip. "I have no idea what I'm doing, blossom. I'll probably fuck it up."

Her smile is smug and satisfied. "No, you won't." She accepts the fresh cocktail from the bartender and sips from the straw.

I stroke my hand down her back. I don't even know what's different—I don't know what this means to her, but I guess I'd better figure it the hell out.

"When you said you'd throat-punch anyone who talked to me here…"

I don't fill in the blank. I don't know where she's going with this.

"Would you?" she asks point blank.

I lift my shoulders. "I might. I could, Kayla. Easily. I think you know what I'm capable of."

"I never asked for nice." She lifts her chin.

A smile flirts around the corners of my mouth. "Master?" I'm asking, not correcting. Is she still my slave? Or now that she pushed me into boyfriend territory, does she think that's over?

She blushes, though. Leans into me, her soft tits brushing against my ribs as she purrs, "I never asked for nice, Master." Sweet as honey.

"Be careful what you green-light, blossom. If it's a boyfriend you want, I'm possessive as hell. Any man who touches you is toast."

A shiver runs through her, but she's got her moon-eyes on. The ones that stare up at me like I'm some kind of hero and not the guy who puts her on her knees and makes her plead for mercy on a regular basis.

7

Kayla

The next morning, we sit on the patio of the Four Seasons, enjoying the California sun and a late brunch. I hate Sundays because it means our time is almost over. He'll fly back to Chicago, and I'll go back to my other life. The one where I'm not a sex slave or the girlfriend to a dangerous criminal. There's such a giant fissure between my twin selves now I can barely straddle it.

I'm also cracked open, with no armor, almost no sense of self at all because Pavel just turned me inside out upstairs.

I came without asking again this morning, so he spread my legs, spanked my pussy with the leather strap and then ate me out until I screamed myself hoarse. I feel so vulnerable after intense sessions like that. His seat across the table from me—less than three feet away—feels way too far. When I reach for his hand, he takes my fingers and caresses them. "Come here," he says, seeming to understand. I stand, and he moves my chair around to the side of the table, right beside him. I scoot it even closer, and drape one of my knees over his.

"You want to go back up to the room for more aftercare?" He's so patient and attentive with me post-scene. I know it's not his usual way, which makes it all the more addictive.

Again, my roommates would say this is dysfunctional.

I rest my head on his shoulder. I know it's ridiculous to be this needy. But I have to lean into Pavel to soak up a sense of safety when I'm this wide open.

My phone rings. I'm going to ignore it until I remember that it could be Lara, and then I lunge for my purse.

It is. I swipe across the screen to answer.

"I got you in, darling," she sing-songs. "It took me all weekend to get someone to take my call, but you're in. The audition is in ninety minutes. I'll text you the address."

"Oh!" I shoot a glance at Pavel, who must have overheard because he nods and throws some bills down on the table. "Great!" My heart's already pounding like I'm at the audition. "I'll be there. Thank you."

Pavel stands the moment I end the call. "You have an audition?" He slides my chair back as I stand, like a gentleman of a bygone time. The behavior is so at odds with his appearance and normal cocky behavior that it makes me a little swoony. But, of course, I'm already in the swooning state.

"Yes, for a television show. This could be my big break." I sound breathless. My heart's still rapping against my ribs like my life is in danger. "I'm sorry, I know this is our last few hours."

"Don't be sorry. I'll drive you."

"Okay." I flash a smile at him, as my excitement mounts. "I'll go change."

I didn't bring audition clothes, and there's probably not enough time to go back to my apartment, so I sort through my suitcase for what I have. I decide to wear the red dress I wore last night, just dressed down with a pair of Converse because it's daytime. It's quirky and hopefully will be memorable to the casting director.

Pavel packs his things and stays out of my way as I spin around the suite, touching up my makeup and hair and packing my suitcase.

"Okay," I say when I'm ready.

"You look perfect." Pavel stacks both our suitcases and takes them with one hand. With the other, he catches my fingers and twines his through them. "You've got this."

We head down in the elevator, and Pavel checks out as I wait for the valet attendant to bring my old car around. Pavel slides behind the wheel and loads the address into his map app on his phone. As the car sails smoothly into traffic, I shiver a little.

"Are you cold?" Pavel turns on the heater and adjusts the vents.

"No, I'm just…"

He takes his eyes away from traffic to look at me.

"I'm freaking out a little bit. I'm nervous. This is usually where I try to channel Sasha because she's not afraid of anything."

Pavel lets out a soft scoff. "Yes, Sasha has a pretty high opinion of herself."

I look at him in surprise. "Do you not like Sasha?"

"Sasha is Sasha." He shrugs. "She's the daughter of my former boss and the wife of a brother. I would kill or die for her."

I blink, stunned by this little glimpse into his world. His loyalty. A code for living. Would he kill or die for me? Remembering his actions at the convenience store, I'm suddenly quite certain he would. And like that night, it turns me on, even as it scares me.

"You two are friends, though, right?"

Pavel shrugs again, like friend isn't a word he would use with Sasha. "Why are you asking?"

I laugh a little at myself then confess, "I've been so jealous of what she has with you."

He scoffs again. "She has nothing with me. She is my annoying housemate. Nothing more." His gaze on me is bemused. "You were jealous? Of Sasha?" He can't seem to believe it.

"She knows you better than I do."

"Ah." He sobers. "I understand." Then he shakes his head. "She knows nothing. You see more of me than I show to anyone else. Don't ever be jealous of another woman."

"Why don't you ever invite me to come to Chicago?"

He gives me a long look. "Because I'm a bastard, and I don't want to share you. But if you want to come, you're invited. Any time, Kayla."

"Okay," I say softly.

"You don't need to be like Sasha for this audition," he says, and I catch a little heat in his gaze. "You're you."

Wings flap in my chest.

"I'm just scared because I don't feel like myself. I still feel … raw from our scene."

"I see." He picks up my fingers and brings them to his mouth, kissing the backs of them. "Use it. I called you *blossom* the night we met because I thought you would be easily crushed, but I was wrong. You *are* a flower—one that blooms under duress. You open wide. That's your superpower, *malysh.* So use it. When you're in that audition, don't try to hide that openness. There's no person on this planet who won't connect with you when you're like that, period. And if you don't get this part, then it's because it wasn't the right one for you, not because you weren't absolutely perfect."

I blink back the wetness in my eyes, my chest warm and glowy from his words. I've been told before to believe it's not me, it's just about the part—we actors tell ourselves this all the time to soothe the sting of rejection. But this time, when Pavel says it, I actually believe it.

He pulls up in front of the building, and I take a deep breath.

"Knock them dead, blossom. Text me when you're done, and I'll pick you up."

"Thank you." I lean over for a kiss. It's awkward because he didn't lean my way or try to touch me, but he cradles my face and kisses me back lightly.

"You've got this."

I step out of the car. I don't know who I am. I don't know up from down. Maybe that's why I believe Pavel implicitly. My defenses are down, and Pavel thinks I'm perfect. All I can do is show up and be me.

Pavel

I don't know how long it will take Kayla, but I figure there's time to take her car to a carwash and get an exterior and interior clean. She hasn't texted by the time it's finished, so I take a chance and bring it to the Jiffy Lube for an oil change and tune up, sliding a hundred dollar bill into the guy in charge's hand to get it done quickly.

Afterward, I drive around L.A., looking at it for the first time. I realize I don't even know where Kayla lives. I was playing fantasy dom—meeting her at Black Light and then bringing her to a hotel room for the weekend.

Now, though, things have shifted.

I see a commercial real estate sign in front of a large apartment complex and some wild and ridiculous notion pops in my head. I pull over to call the number on the sign.

"This is Larry," a guy practically yells over the phone. Sounds like he's driving a convertible.

"Yeah, just wondering the selling price for the property on Wilmont."

"Are you an agent?" he demands.

"No. This is Pavel Pushkin. I'm a real estate investor from Chicago."

It's five million, eight. I won't show it until you've proven you have funding."

I ignore his last statement. "How many units?"

"Six one-bedroom units and six two. The top floor is a penthouse suite, and there's a pool on the roof."

"How big are the units?"

"Eight hundred square feet and one thousand."

"I'll be in touch," I say and end the call without a thank you. Groveling isn't my thing.

I stare at the building and run the numbers in my head.

Real estate is the true secret to Ravil's wealth. He may run smuggling and gambling and loan shark operations—staples of the bratva business—but he invested his money wisely. Somehow, he made enough—or maybe he killed the right people to inherit enough—to buy the Kremlin—lakefront property in Chicago. Definitely worth multiple millions. And now, with his beautiful new crime-intolerant wife, Ravil has steered the organization in a relatively legit direction. He can because he's now a real estate mogul, not a crime lord.

I wonder, briefly, if Igor bankrolled him. I never asked because it's none of my business.

All this time, I've saved all my earnings, so when things

have cooled down enough to return to Moscow, I could get myself set up somehow. Oh, I'd still work for the bratva. The only way out of the bratva is in a box, or so they say. But having my own business—sanctioned by the *pakhan*, of course—has been my goal.

Sasha just inherited something like sixty million when Igor died. I wonder if she could be talked into backing me on something like this?

But that's a crazy thought. Why would I start a business venture in Los Angeles if I'm moving to Moscow?

Well, the why is pretty obvious.

I'm thinking with my dick.

But my mother's alone in Russia. Friendless, isolated, depressed.

Because of what I did.

So giving any thought to not returning would make me even more heartless than everyone thinks I am.

Blyad'.

A text comes through on my phone from Kayla, and I put the car back in drive and swing in front of the building where she auditioned to pick her up.

There's a calmness around her as she walks out that hits me square in the chest. It's not the kind of hair-tossing confidence Sasha wields, but she looks grounded. Happy.

I get out to open the door for her, and she leans into me, lifting her face with a smile and big moon eyes. "You're awfully nice to your slave," she purrs.

"My slave earned it." I brush her cheek with my thumb. "How'd it go?"

She exhales with a smile. "Really well. As good as it could have. I did a couple scenes for them, and one made me tear up. It was perfect, honestly. Thanks for the pep talk before I went in. It really helped."

"You don't need pep talks, little flower. You already have it all. Believe that."

She keeps leaning against me, her tits pressing soft against my ribs. My dick twitches against my zipper at the contact. I want to throw her over my shoulder, run back into that building and find some supply closet where I can fuck her brains out one last time before I go.

As if she's reading my mind, she asks, "What time's your flight?"

I shrug. "I already missed it. I'm sure I can find another one going out tonight."

"Do you want me to take you to the airport?"

This is new, too. We've always just met at Black Light or the hotel. When it's over, I take a cab or rideshare, and she drives away.

I know I should tell her no. That I'll call a ride share. There's something desperate and clingy about us needing to stay together until the last possible minute.

But the fact is, I do want these last few moments with her. Even after a solid forty-eight hours and more orgasms than I can count, it's never enough. There's something thoroughly addictive about Kayla that makes me want to change every plan I've ever made.

I brush my lips over hers. "Yeah. That would be nice. Thanks."

8

Pavel

I get up from the red leather couch in the living room of the penthouse.

"Too much of a chick flick?" Story asks. She's curled up in Oleg's lap on the other end of the sofa. She picked the movie playing on the television—*The Spy Who Dumped Me*. Nikolai's in the chair beside us.

"Nah. It's fine." Although it's true, now that we have three women in the house, our television diet has changed significantly.

"It's stupid," Nikolai says, then holds his hands up when Oleg glares. "I just mean why would you torture someone that way? It doesn't make sense."

"You're just sad you can't wear a leotard while you question captives," his twin, Dima counters. He's at his makeshift desk—a table in the middle of the living room—because he likes to work where all the action is. Or because he can't stop working. The guy would probably combust if he wasn't sitting in front of a computer for at least twelve hours a day.

I haven't seen Ravil, Lucy and the baby since dinner, and Maxim's fucking Sasha's brains out, based on the rhythmic sound of furniture banging against a wall in their room.

"I'll probably be back," I say. "I'm going to make a phone call."

"I think the correct term is video-dom," Nikolai wise-cracks. "Show me your breasts, little slave," he mimics.

One of these assholes overheard me once when I was talking to Kayla, and now I'm fair game.

"I'm calling my mother," I growl and point at Nikolai. "I fucking dare you to make a joke with that."

He holds up his hands in surrender. "Wasn't going to touch it."

"You'd better not."

Dima lifts his head and opens his mouth, but when I glower his way, he closes it again. "Yeah, me neither."

"I'll probably be back." I walk out the front door of the suite and down the elevator hall to my bedroom, which doesn't connect to the main penthouse. It suits me to have a little privacy, since I'm not the most social of the bunch.

I've been itchy and restless this week. The life I adored, revered for the past few years, suddenly seems basic. There's been no one to beat down or torture. Working out and watching television on the couch with my suitemates used to be enough on the off-hours. Now it's mundane.

Kayla's all I can think of, but this week, it's not just about the things I want to do to her. How to torture her. Planning ways to make her scream. Shopping for implements and toys. This week, I'm remembering the things we talked about.

Kayla, I'm not saying no. That's how I shifted from dom to boyfriend in a heartbeat. Because I'm incapable of saying no to that girl, especially when those big blue eyes fill with tears.

And yes, I would be video-domming her tonight if she wasn't working a promotion with her housemates.

When I'm in my bedroom, I pull my phone out and call my mom back.

"Pavel! Are you home from your trip? How is the girl?" she asks in Russian.

"She's good. She lives in Los Angeles. I was visiting her."

"But how do you know her? What is she doing there? What's her name?"

"Her name is Kayla. I met her at an event in Los Angeles. She's an actress. I've been going to visit her on the weekends."

"You're serious about her." My mother sounds surprised.

Not half as surprised as I am. I make a non-committal sound.

I'm serious about tying her up and licking her pussy until she screams...

I clear my throat. "How are you, Mama?"

"Oh, you know…"

"Have you left the apartment? Seen anyone?"

"No."

"You should get out," I say, but I know she won't. She's afraid. My father never let her out of his sight while he was alive. She wouldn't even know how to go out and build a life. She needs support.

Briefly, my thoughts go to Nadia, Adrian's sister. She was brought to this country under horrible circumstances —as a sex slave. Adrian tracked her here and burned down the building where she was being held. Then he worked on taking his revenge for what happened to her.

Unfortunately, the bastard Leon Poval, the Ukrainian slaver, is still at large.

But the point is, Adrian got her help. She video conferences a counselor back in Russia. She feels safe here in the Kremlin where everyone speaks Russian. She's starting to get out. Hell, Adrian even brought her out to one of Story's band's shows last weekend after she met Story and her brother and the rest of the band rehearsing in the building.

"Mama, I'm moving you to the United States."

"*Nyet.*" She doesn't hesitate. I'm not surprised by her refusal.

"*Da.* Everyone in this building speaks Russian. You can make friends. We'll find you something to do—babysit children, or assist Svetlana, the midwife, maybe. Something to keep you busy. I think it would be good for you."

"I don't know…"

It's better than another outright refusal.

"Please, Mama. I'd like to have you closer to me, so I can look after you."

"I don't need looking after."

"Well, I miss your honey cake. You could make it for me. And we will get together for dinner."

She makes a non-committal sound, which I take as a good sign.

"Think about it. I'll arrange things on my end."

"Well…"

"It will be good for you. I'll fly out and get you. If you hate it, I'll fly you back. Yes?"

"Maybe."

"Good," I say. "I'll get you a passport and start the paperwork. I love you, Mama."

"I love you, Pavel." My mother sounds sad, but that's

nothing new. What's new is this idea that I might be able to do something about it.

"Goodbye, Mama. I'll call soon."

"Yes, call soon," she echoes distantly as I end the call.

I end the call and slap the back of the phone into my open palm a few times, considering. I need to talk to Ravil about my idea.

I exit my room and walk back into the suite, heading down the hall to the left toward Ravil's wing. Hearing Benjamin fussing behind their door, I figure it's safe to knock.

"Come in." Lucy, the venerable defense attorney and Ravil's new wife, sits in her glider in their room attempting to nurse the baby.

I look away because even though Lucy's not modest, I figure Ravil would kill me if he thought I was looking at his wife's breasts. "Is Ravil around?" I ask.

The baby latches onto her breast and starts sucking noisily. Lucy's face goes soft with love for her baby. "In his office." She speaks softly, but Benjamin still pops off her nipple to crane his neck and look at me.

I hold my hand up. "Sorry to interrupt."

"It's fine. He's been either fussing or nursing all day. Another growth spurt, I think."

I'm not a baby person. Total understatement. I don't know if I've held that baby more than twice since he was born, and I live with him. But I'm suddenly struck by the vision of Kayla nursing our baby, and a strange form of yearning comes over me.

Blyad'. I've got it bad.

I head into Ravil's office and knock on the door. He's sitting behind his desk, looking at something on his laptop. His gaze is predictably cool. I learned everything I know about mastering a situation from him.

I enter, shoving my hands in my pockets and leaning in the doorframe. "May I interrupt?"

"Yes. Come in."

I don't come in. I stay where I am. Maybe because I'm not fully committed to what I'm asking. I don't even know if it's the right thing to do. Or if my reasons for doing it are pure.

"I was thinking about moving my mother to America. To live here." I drop that bomb and watch it land.

Ravil raises his brows. He knows my history. Why Igor sent me to America. "All right."

"She doesn't speak English. I don't know if I could get her to learn it, either. But we have a nice community here."

Ravil's lips twitch. "I'm sorry, did you just say the words *nice community?*"

My lips quirk in return. "Not that I've ever participated in it. But you know, I thought my mom might find some friends here."

"Sure."

"You'd let her live in the Kremlin?"

"Of course."

"Thank you." I push away from the door frame but hesitate before I leave. "I'm just curious—have you ever let anyone go?"

It's a vague question, but Ravil knows exactly what I mean. "The only way out of the brotherhood is in a box," he tells me. Of course, I know that. It's bratva code.

Except he's broken the code himself. He took a wife, which is forbidden, and he allowed Maxim to remain in the cell after he married.

"What about… sending a brother to a new location? Like how Igor sent you here to the United States?"

Ravil lifts a brow. "Igor sent me here for a good reason —to set up a smuggling route. I would have to have a good reason to diminish the numbers of the Chicago Bratva. Especially those in my inner circle."

Well, fuck.

I don't give up, though. Ravil can be a hardass, but underneath is an unmatched benevolence. "I can't decide if you're giving me a hard time to watch me sweat or you're shutting me down completely," I tell him.

Ravil has a champion poker face—nothing shows at all in his expression. But then he says, "No one is going to hand you the life you want, Pavel. You have to take it."

My pulse picks up at the challenge. Am I going to take it? The life I want? Kayla, as mine forever?

"Let's say I wished to relocate—not back to Moscow. To stay in your cell, but operate in a different city. Would you let me set up an operation there? Paying my dues and answering to you, of course?"

"I'm not going to discuss hypothetical situations. When you make your choice, we'll discuss your fate with the organization."

I stare at him for a long moment, trying to decipher the meaning of his words. In the end, I decide he's giving me permission. Because I can't believe he'd put a bullet in my head without a clear warning, and this was murky as fuck. He means we'll negotiate terms.

He means yes. I give a mental fist pump.

"Thank you."

He nods.

"*Spasibo*," I repeat my thanks in Russian because I feel so much fucking gratitude I almost smile—a very rare occurrence for me.

Kayla

I venture into the kitchen with a towel wrapped under my armpits to grab a can of soda. I have an audition this afternoon before my weekend with Pavel.

"You look great," I tell my roommate Kimberly, who is dressed in a pair of short-shorts with fishnets underneath and a child-sized red T-shirt with the name of a new energy drink across her tits.

"You should be going with us," she complains. Normally I would be dressed in the same shirt, going out with my three roommates. We're a promotions team. Or we were. But most promotions fall on Friday afternoons or evenings, which means I've missed seven out of the last nine events. "I don't know how you're going to pay the rent when you've barely worked in a month," she says.

I get it. They feel let down. Maybe they miss me. It's not like they can't do the jobs without me. Jagger, the company owner, just finds another woman to fill in for me.

"Well, I have enough to get by." I don't want to tell her that Pavel's been giving me money. I don't want them inferring that he's paying me for sex. They already think our relationship is bizarre.

Kimberly puts her hands on her hips. At five foot ten and in six-inch heels, she towers over me. I'm barely over five feet, but as my agent likes to say, I make up for the size in talent and hard work. That's the pitch, anyway. "How long is this thing going to keep going?" she demands, and I bristle.

I'm usually the peace-maker around here. The one who makes sure everyone's getting along, and there's enough ice cream in the fridge when we all get our periods in the same week and are at each other's throats.

"How long is my *relationship* going to keep going?"

She turns away, like she doesn't want to show me the

scorn on her face. "Right. Of course, you don't know." Her voice has softened. She pities me.

Now I'm really pissed.

"Kayla, we're just worried about you," she says in the new, soft tone, turning back to face me with big, sympathetic eyes.

"*We*?"

"Yeah, we," Ashley says from behind me. She's dressed in a matching outfit, only she's cut the t-shirt up so it shows more skin. "We're just concerned. I mean, I get you want to explore your fantasies, and this guy does that for you, but it seems like it's consuming you."

My chest and eyes get hot. I rewrap the towel around me to try to garner my thoughts.

Sheri, my third roommate, shows up in the kitchen wearing a similar kind, sympathetic expression. Jeez, it's like a goddamn intervention.

"You, too?" I demand.

She shrugs. "I'm not judging—I mean, I'm the queen of bad relationships."

Understatement. Sheri has a knack for finding guys who took off their wedding rings to get her in bed. Cheaters seem to look at her and know she'd be the perfect diversion.

"Who said this was a bad relationship?" My voice sounds shrill to my ears.

"You're seeing a guy who gets off on hurting you. I get that it's consensual, but it does raise some major red flags, don't you think?" Kimberly doesn't hold back.

"No. Why?"

"Well, is it just sex? I mean, what is it?" Ashley pulls out a chair and plops down at the kitchen table like we're going to sit and talk about this.

Oh, hell no.

"It just seems like you're investing a lot of your time into something that isn't going anywhere," Sheri agrees, also taking a seat.

"Right. I thought it was going to be over at the end of your free month at Black Light," Kimberly says.

"Well, it wasn't," I say with false cheer. "It *is* going somewhere." I shrug my shoulders, catching my towel when the action dislodges it, and sail from the kitchen to my room. I'm an actress, faking it is my game, not that they won't see through it. You can't live and work with three best friends without them knowing you inside and out.

Our relationship is deepening, but if he's moving back to Moscow, I'm setting myself up for a heartbreak.

Sheri follows me into my bedroom and sits on the bed. I drop the towel and pull on a pair of panties because we aren't shy around here.

"I'm sorry," Sheri says. "That wasn't supposed to feel like an ambush. Did it?"

"Kind of." I stand in my closet, pulling out possible outfits for the audition. "I'm just wondering… like, where do you want things to go with this guy?"

I throw a half-dozen choices of clothing on my bed and sigh, pretending to consider them, but really considering the question. "I want him," I admit. "I want what Sasha has."

Our former roommate, Sasha's father ran the Russian mafia before he died last fall. In some medieval and backwards move, he arranged a marriage for Sasha to Maxim, one of his bratva men who lives in Chicago. We first met him when she ran away from her new husband and went out on the town with us.

I sort of got the bug for a dominant, powerful Russian man like him in my life. When she introduced me to Pavel later, I wanted him the moment I met him. The fact that he didn't want me just made him all the more appealing.

"Well, Maxim is hot. But is that what Pavel wants? I mean, you guys don't even live in the same city. Where is this thing going?"

She's right. It can't go much further. And yet it feels like it will.

"I just wonder how much of this is fantasy and how much is real," Sheri says.

I want to flip my wet hair and say something glib and confident, but Sheri's sifting through my shirts, helping me to pick the right one. She's being a friend, and friends are honest with one another. Which means I have to be honest with myself.

"Me too," I admit. I take one of the blouses she holds out to me and put it on, turning in a circle for her to see the full effect. "But I'm starting to get to know him—beyond just the master-dom role. I don't know—I really like this guy."

Sheri surveys me then shakes her head, wordlessly handing me a different top.

"The problem is more that I don't think he can move here, and I'm not leaving L.A. So it can't go anywhere."

"Right. That's my concern for you, too. It seems like you're already in deep with this guy. You're giving up all your work shifts to see him, and there's no potential for a future. "Also, you're sad every Monday when the weekend is over. We hate seeing you that way."

I hate that she's right.

"I mean if you love the kinky sex, go for it. But do you have to see him every weekend? It seems a little intense. What if you just saw him once a month or something?"

It makes perfect sense. I do miss working the promotions with my friends. I'm not exercising as much as I should because I skip all weekend, and I've lost focus on my career. Pavel has become my focus.

My extremely hot, very dominant focus.

One that I'm not willing to give up, even for one weekend.

9

Kayla

I drive through the gates and park my car in front of Director Blake Ensign's Hollywood mansion and pull my mirror down to check my make-up again. This is it—the biggest audition I've ever had.

Apparently Ensign is leaving for Europe tomorrow and wanted to get this part—a leading role—cast before he left. The casting director scheduled twenty-seven call-backs, all at his mansion for his convenience since he's leaving town. The simple fact that I get to see the inside of Blake Ensign's house makes it feel like I've finally arrived.

And I'm auditioning for a leading role!

It finally feels like things might be happening for me. Maybe Pavel was right—my dreams will come true.

I head to the door, where I'm met by an assistant with a clipboard. "Name?" She doesn't even look at me.

"Kayla Winstead."

She finds my name on her clipboard and makes a checkmark. "You can wait in the living room. Mr. Ensign is seeing people in his office one at a time. He's running about two hours late.

Gah. Two hours late. Pavel will be waiting for me at the Four Seasons.

"Can I get you some water?"

"Um, yes, please. Thanks, that would be great."

My heart is already pounding, and I'm only meeting the assistant.

"Water," she calls out to what must be her assistant and ushers me into a giant living room area. The floor is some kind of expensive tile, and the domed ceiling is vaulted—at least forty feet high. Great marble pillars define the perimeter.

"Hi," I say nervously to the six other women waiting. Two I recognize from other casting calls. Only one answers me with a "Hello." All of them look like I do—petite, blonde, early twenties.

My looks aren't enough to land this job, not that they ever have been here in L.A. Back in high school, in Wisconsin, they got me every acting and modeling job I tried out for. But here—I'm the proverbial small fish in a very big sea.

I pull out my phone to text Pavel. *I'm so sorry—I'm at a casting call that may run late.*

He doesn't reply, but he's probably in the air already.

I put my phone away to do some deep breathing and get centered.

Nearly three hours later, I get called in. I'm the last one for the day, and it's already 5:30 p.m. Pavel will already be waiting for me at the hotel—not that I can think about that now.

I draw a steadying breath and walk in.

Blake Ensign is not behind his desk, but on a loveseat.

He's in beachwear—shorts and a Tommy Bahama type shirt. One bare foot is crossed over his knee.

"All right, come in. You're the last one, right?"

"Yes." I look around, not sure where to stand. Or do I sit? I have no idea how this works.

"Read the lines," he commands with a wave.

I stand directly in front of him and hold the script. I had enough time to memorize the part while I was waiting, but I'm afraid I'll screw up, so I keep it at the ready, my trembling fingers making the papers shake.

He reads the male part in a monotone voice, and I pick up my lines. They don't come out nearly as well as they sounded rehearsing in my head in the living room. Nothing like the way they sounded at the first casting call.

Still, I give it my best, making it through a couple pages before he stops me.

"All right, Kayla. That's enough."

I screwed the pooch on this one.

"I'm sorry—I'm just nervous. I did a much better job at the first audition. Can I try it again?"

"Come here." He crooks a finger at me.

I walk closer, but he keeps beckoning. I stop when my toes hit his, then sort of look around, trying to figure out where he wants me. To sit beside him? Kneel at his feet? "I'm a very hard worker. If you give me a shot, I will do everything it takes to please you."

As it turns out, my choice of words were all wrong.

Ensign sits back and adjusts his cock like I just gave him a boner. No—he's not adjusting it. He's holding it. Squeezing it.

Oh God—I can't take my eyes away!

My heart hammers in my chest.

"Everything it takes, hmm?" he says, his voice suggesting. "I like that in an actress. One of the most important characteristics, really."

Oh my God. I'm going to #MeToo right now. This is not happening. Please no.

He catches my wrist and tugs my hand down to his dick, covering my fingers to make me squeeze it.

Oh shit. Oh shit, oh shit, oh shit.

I don't know what to do. I mean, I do. I slap his face and leave. Right?

Of course, that's what I should do. But burning bridges in Hollywood would be a terrible mistake. So I need to get out of this nicely. If that's possible.

"Show me how you'd please me," he says.

I want to barf. Literally. The contents of my empty stomach churn as I pull my hand away.

I stumble back. "With my talent," I say quickly. I will please you with my talent. I p-promise."

"Yes, and I'd like to experience that talent right now." He says it like he's totally sure of himself. Like every other actress who came in sucked him off.

Did they?

Or am I just the lucky one at the end of the day?

Wait—why am I evening wondering? It doesn't matter—I just need to get myself out of this.

"Well, that's not…" I try to swallow. "I need to go. I'm sorry this isn't going to work…" I make a beeline for the door.

"You sure? I could open a lot of doors for you, Kayla Winstead."

I hate myself for even hesitating. I mean, I really, truly hate myself. But that's how bad I want this dream.

Tears prick my eyes as I turn. "Thanks, but I'd rather get there a different way."

Why did I even thank him? Seriously. What is wrong with me?

I throw the door open and stumble out, ignoring the assistant, who is on her phone, and the assistant's assistant, who is also on his phone.

I throw open the front door and run out, straight to my car. Once I'm in it, I back out as quickly as I can. It's not until I'm on the road driving that I break down into sobs.

I need to talk to a friend. I could call one of my roommates, but something makes me call Sasha, instead. She's the strongest woman I know. She'll make me feel better.

The moment she answers, she hears me sniffing. "Kayla? What is it? Did Pavel do something? I will kill him."

"No, it's not Pavel. I'm supposed to be with him right now, but…"

"But what? What's going on?" Sasha's Russian accent gets thicker with urgency.

"I just got...casting couched." I sniff.

"Aw, fuck!" Sasha has the cutest way of saying fuck. I love her accent. "What happened? Are you okay? You should go to the police."

I suck in a breath. "No. I don't want to go to the police. Nothing actually happened. I mean, he didn't force himself on me or anything. It was just sexual harassment. He wanted me to give him a blowjob to prove how far I'd go to please him."

"What a dick! I'm so sorry that happened to you. God, don't tell Pavel, he will literally kill the guy."

I sniff but my sobs subside as I suddenly focus on her words. "Um, when you say *literally*…"

"I mean...seriously, Kayla—Pavel will kill him. Like shoot him in the head and kill him. Bratva men are serious about protecting their women."

My pulse races. “I… I can’t let that happen. He already told me he’s wanted for murder in Russia. At least, I think that’s what he implied.”

“Really? I didn’t know. But that’s how it’s supposed to be—we’re not supposed to know such things. Honestly, I don’t think I’d tell him if I were you. He’s going to want vengeance. Pavel is not a forgiving guy, I know that much about him.”

I mop my tears with one hand while steering with the other. I probably shouldn’t be driving in the state I’m in.

“I think you should #MeToo him on social media,” Sasha declares. “It could win you sympathy points and get you other casting calls. You know—use this to your advantage while shaming the hell out of him.”

“I don’t know…” I say slowly. I still fear getting blacklisted.

“Yeah, actually, Pavel could see it, and that could backfire. Nevermind. Bad idea. And, I mean, if you want Pavel to kill him—I’m not judging. It could be nice having your warrior slay dragons for you.”

“No,” I say quickly. “God, no. I would never want to be the reason he killed. I mean, I don’t want any of that.”

“Of course you don’t. Well, maybe cancel with Pavel for this weekend if you’re not up to seeing him. Tell him you’re sick. He doesn’t have to get his dick sucked every single weekend, right?”

For some reason, the thought of not seeing Pavel sends a whirlwind of anxiety rushing through me.

“No, I’m okay. I’m an actress. I know how to change my mood—or fake it.”

“Are you sure? I mean, I think you need a big hug right now, not Pavel domming you around.”

Actually, the thought of diving straight into that role—the fantasy role where all I have to do is surrender—sounds perfect. "No, I'm good. Thanks for talking me through this. I knew there was a reason I called you and not Ashley or Kimberly."

"All right. Virtual hug to you. Call me again if you want to talk more, okay?"

"I will, thanks." I end the call just as I pull into the valet parking for the Four Seasons. I tug the mirror down and wipe under my eyes. I look like crap, but maybe I can tell Pavel I need a shower first. He knows I'm coming straight from an audition that ran long.

Squaring my shoulders, I take my bag from the trunk and enter the hotel. I practice my smile, trying to lighten my mood. Whatever I do, I can't let Pavel know the truth.

Pavel

I stand on the balcony of the hotel room, trying to unclench my fingers. Kayla's hours late and hasn't responded to my last couple texts checking in. The need to get in a car and drive somewhere very fast to make sure she's unharmed spikes about every five minutes, but of course, I don't know where to drive.

Damn. I should've put a tracker in her phone like Ravil and Maxim did with their women. I chose not to because I already control so many aspects of Kayla's life, plus it felt like a betrayal of trust. She gives herself freely, and she wouldn't lie. My enemies are in Chicago, not here, so I didn't think her safety was at issue. Why would I need to track her?

My phone beeps with an incoming text. *Just got here. I'm so sorry, Master, the audition went really long.*

Thank fuck. I release the breath I didn't know I was holding and step inside. I want to go down and meet her, to carry her bag, but I'm not sure which way she's coming, so I wait until she knocks on the door.

I open it, all set to give her a cool command to take off her clothes when I realize her mood is all wrong. She avoids my gaze, ducking her head as she passes me. I pick up her suitcase and bring it to the rack.

"I'm so sorry I'm late." She still barely meets my gaze. Fuck—are her eyes red?

What in the hell happened?

I catch her hips and turn her to fully face me. "Hey," I say softly, waiting for her to settle under my hands. Under my gaze.

But she doesn't.

"What happened?"

She turns out of my grasp to face her suitcase. "Nothing. Just a bad audition, that's all. And I was stressed because I knew you were waiting."

I want to tell her I was fine, that she didn't need to stress over me, but something doesn't ring right. I've had too much practice beating the truth out of liars. She's a good actress, but something's off, and it's not just her lack of submission.

"Hey." I stay where I am. "Turn around."

She freezes, another tell. Prickles crawl up the back of my neck. What in the fuck is going on? When she turns around, her eyes have the wide rabbit look, but more scared than eager to please. I don't like this version of it.

"Did you just lie to me?" My words seem to take all the oxygen out of the room. There's a plummeting sensation, like we're in an elevator dropping quickly.

"Pavel…" Again, not the right response.

I go cold all over. Alarms go off, but I don't even know what they mean. "Why did you lie?" My voice is so soft, it's barely more than a whisper.

"I *did* have a bad audition," she insists.

I believe her, but I wait because I know there's something she's trying to hide.

"W-what makes you think I'm lying?"

Gospodi, now she's really freaking me out. I step into her space and cup her chin, trying to will whatever's in her brain out of that pretty mouth.

"I detect lies for a living," I tell her. We stare at each other for a moment. Her pulse is frantic at her throat. I can't decide if this is a dom moment or a boyfriend moment. Do I threaten punishment if she won't talk? I settle for the minced, "Come clean."

"I got casting-couched. The director wanted me to suck his dick to show how much I wanted the part."

My nostrils flare, and I let out a string of curses in Russian. That man will pay. But… "Why didn't you want me to know?"

"I just—" She stops herself from speaking and swallows. She's still hiding something again.

A massive alarm goes off in my head. Everything flashes hot and cold as my brows slam down. "Wait… did you do it?"

Her outrage couldn't be faked. She slaps my face hard, and relief flushes through me.

"Sorry." I catch her wrist and bring her fingers to my lips to kiss them. "I'm sorry, Kayla. Of course, you didn't." I shake my head, still trying to make sense of it. "It's just that you lied straight to my face. It scared the shit out of me."

Her eyes swim with tears.

"Why didn't you want me to know? What did he do?"

She still resists, lowering her chin and drawing back a little.

I rub my hands up and down her arms as if she were cold. "What's his name?"

Kayla shakes her head.

"No?" I didn't mean to put a dangerous edge on the word, but she draws back at my tone, and her ass hits the suitcase. I still have her wrist, which I use to steady her.

She wets her lips. "Sasha said you'd kill him."

I let out a humorless chuff of laughter as her reluctance to be forthright suddenly makes perfect sense. But then the notion that Sasha thinks I will kill this guy—that he deserves to die for what he did to her—sharpens the ruthless part of me to a lethal point.

"His name." It's a command, and she doesn't miss the tone.

She swallows. "Are you going to kill him?"

"Did he touch you?" This man is fucking dead if he did.

She shakes her head repeatedly but then says. "He...he put my hand on his cock—o-over his shorts. But when I pulled away, he let me go."

I nod slowly, considering what I'm going to do with this cocksucker.

"Does that mean *yes*, you're going to kill him?"

I draw in a slow breath then shake my head. Kayla doesn't want me to. Her soul's too pure to have that on her conscience. "What do you want me to do?"

Her expression is uncertain. "Please don't kill him."

I consider and nod. "If you don't want him dead, I'll respect that. You have my word. But I am going to make sure you're the last woman he tries this shit on."

I wait for her to soften, then I slowly draw her into my arms. "Are you okay, little flower? You swear that's all that happened?" She wraps her arms around my waist, pressing her face to my chest. I kiss the top of her head. When she doesn't answer, I say, "Talk to me."

"I'm okay. It was upsetting, but I'm fine. And you're here."

The last three words do something foreign to my heart.

"Tell me what you need."

She lifts her head and peers up at me. She's soft and supple and totally submissive again. "Just you," she murmurs. "Us. To be your slave tonight."

"Hm." I tip her chin up, drinking in her unconditional surrender like it's the fuel that keeps me alive. The electricity sparks between us and a haze of filthy ideas flash through my head. "You definitely have a punishment coming for lying to me. But I'm going to feed you and make sure you're all right first."

Her eyes dilate, and her nipples poke through her red scoop-neck blouse. "I'm not hungry yet. Honestly. I just want to play."

"Come here." I take her hand and lead her into the bathroom where I turn on the shower. "Strip."

She's instantly eager, kicking off her heels, shimmying out of her top and slacks. I lean back against the counter to watch her bra and panties come off, my dick lengthening in my pants.

"Wash off your day, blossom. Take your time."

"Yes, Master," she murmurs, head bowed.

I marvel at my urge to kiss that bowed head. How affectionate she's taught me to be in just a few short weeks. That first night at Black Light, after I broke her as I'd known I would, the urge to walk away—hell, to run away was so strong. But Maxim directed me back to her. Said I owned her now. That she was mine. And that weight, that responsibility felt so light and heavy at the same time. I'd never held a woman before that night. I'd fucked. I'd scened with some women, though I was new to the BDSM world. But Kayla curled up in a blanket in my arms, needed to be held, and it forever changed me.

Whatever it is that she calls up in me is what makes me unwilling to walk away. This relationship is impractical at best—probably unhealthy for her, yet I'm here for the seventh weekend, more invested in seeing her again than I am in my next breath.

I stay where I am and watch through the glass shower doors, enjoying the view for a bit, then head into the bedroom to prepare for our scene.

This is the part that disturbs me. How excited I am to hurt Kayla. How hard I get when she whimpers, when she pleads. How much the idea of punishing her, then soothing it all away makes me feel like a mountain.

The justifications I have in my head—that she wants this, that she asked for it, that she enjoys it, too, only go so far. She just had an upsetting experience at her audition. Bad enough to make her cry. Should I really go through with this?

But she said it's what she wanted. She seemed excited. And she has a safe word. I keep reminding myself of that. She has a safe word, and she doesn't want me reminding her that she's free to walk out that door any time she wants.

So it's up to me to figure out how to give her what she needs.

I prepare for our scene.

The water in the shower turns off. Kayla doesn't dally. In just a few minutes, she walks out of the bathroom, her naked body flushed from the heat of the shower. I watch her from the armchair by the sliding glass doors as she comes to me, stealing a glance at the implements and pillows I laid out on the bed before she kneels at my feet.

I take a mental snapshot of yet another magnificent picture. Kayla's wet hair falls over her shoulders, sending rivulets of water trailing over her puckered nipples. She sits on her heels, her open thighs inviting my fingers to stroke between her legs to find out just how wet it makes her to submit to me.

"I'm sorry for lying, Master," she murmurs.

I doubt either one of us is very sorry now. But I do want to make this point. I nearly choked on my heart for a minute there thinking we were over. Not understanding why she would ever try to deceive me.

"Thank you." I don't touch her—not yet, even though I can see she wants it. She leans forward, her pretty face tilted up, those eyes trained on my face. "Don't keep things from me again, blossom. I don't lie to you; I expect the same respect. We don't lie to each other."

Her chin wobbles. "Yes, Master."

"Listen, I don't want you scared of me. I like to run the show, but that doesn't mean I won't respect your wishes."

She blinks. "What if I wished you to not do anything?"

Blyad'. She wants me to give this guy a pass? No fucking way. "*Nyet.* Someone puts their hands on you, they're going to answer to me, end of story. You're mine, Kayla. That means I protect you to the death."

She shifts her butt on her heels, like that turned her on. "Yes, Master." Her voice is soft and honey-sweet.

I unzip my jeans. "Show me you're sorry."

10

Kayla

A shudder of pleasure runs through Pavel when I lick around the head of his cock and then take him into my mouth. I love sucking Pavel's dick. I love how submissive it makes me feel, how glorious the ultimate act of service is. This time, though, I'm determined to make it the best blowjob of his life. I'm a pleaser. I hate feeling like he's disappointed in me, and the need to get out of trouble and earn his praise drives me to use everything in my arsenal. I take him deeper than I have before, going slowly to practice relaxing my gag reflex until I get his full length into my throat.

His hand fists in my hair, but he makes no sounds. This guy always holds himself back. It makes me try all the harder. Sometimes I wonder if a guy was just nice to me, I'd be bored. I'm certainly never attracted to the nice guys.

Not that Pavel is mean. He's attentive, and there's an outline of respect even when he's being completely disrespectful. He takes care of my needs. He's just… not nice.

But who cares? Some of us like rough. There's nothing wrong with that, no matter what my roommates think.

I suck hard, drawing my mouth slowly back, listening for Pavel's harsh intake of breath, sensing the tightening of his fingers in my hair. I wait long enough to create urgency before I take all of him back into my mouth, into my throat. He lets out a groan.

I'm wet just from his pleasure, from my subservient act, from taking on the role of slave.

Pavel's breath grows ragged as he starts to gently guide my head, and then eventually takes over, directing the action with his fist in my hair.

I nearly come myself when he chokes and then groans, shooting his essence down my throat. The salty taste burns a little, and I pull back to swallow. I wipe my face with the back of my hand. "Master?" I chose this moment strategically. He's always more generous after he comes or after he's broken me.

He looks at me with those cool, grey eyes. I know I pleased him because he just got off, but it doesn't show in his face.

When he doesn't answer, I rush forward, "Can I be over your knee for my punishment?" I saw he'd laid out pillows in the center of the bed, and I know exactly how he intends to use them, but I would so much rather have the intimacy of being over his lap—being close to him, especially because this is real punishment. At least I think it is. It's so hard to tell if anything's real with Pavel.

My emotions are real—that's what matters. I'm already close to breaking, and he hasn't even started. I crave connection.

"Is that what you need?" He brushes his thumb across my lower lip, and my body responds like he's a musician bowing my strings.

"Please, Master."

"*Da.* Come here." He tucks his cock away and stands, lifting me by my wrists to stand. He walks to his suitcase and pulls out a small pocket paddle—the kind that's round like a small ping pong paddle, just big enough to strike one buttcheek. He hasn't used it on me before, and a shiver of mingled excitement and fear runs up my spine.

He walks the edge of the bed and sits, tugging me over one knee, my torso resting on the bed. "Take a pillow, blossom."

I reach for one of the pillows piled in the center of the bed and hug it under my chest, resting my cheek on it.

He spanks me with his hand. The first few slaps are hard—hard enough to take my breath away. He delivers five and then stops, reaching for something. I brace myself for whatever he has planned. I relax when I sense something hard and rounded at the entrance of my sex. He pushes in a small bullet vibrator and turns it onto low.

I'm already dripping with desire, and the vibrator has the effect of waking up my entire pelvic region. My next exhale has a moan to it. Pavel doesn't stop with filling my pussy. He spreads my cheeks and drops a dollop of lube on my anus. I gasp, tightening against the surprise sensation.

Pavel rolls the rounded end of a stainless steel buttplug against my asshole then pushes in.

I squeak at the pressure.

"Take it," he growls.

I work hard to relax, forcing out a slow exhale and gradually releasing the tension in my sphincter muscles. As soon as they go slack, he pushes in. It's a crazy mixture of pleasure and pain—the ring of muscles stretching open burns, but the sensation is counteracted by the buzzing against my G-spot and the internal fullness as the plug enters my body and finally seats.

I whimper, feeling fully surrendered now, fully his. The position is humiliating but hot. There's something I adore about my entire body being owned and controlled by my demanding lover.

"Please," I mewl, even though I don't know what I'm begging for.

Certainly not for him to stop. I know he won't. And not for more, either. The sensations are already too much—I'm on overload.

But he does give me more. He starts spanking me again with both holes full. Every spank jiggles the plug inside my ass, sending fresh bursts of sensation through me while the vibrator takes me right to the edge.

"Master, please," I plead. Now I understand what I was begging for. "I need to come."

Already.

I need to come desperately. And I'm almost certain he will refuse.

"No." The syllable is harsh—a rebuke for even asking.

His spanks fall fast and hard, lighting up my ass and making my back muscles tense.

"Please, Master." I'm not really asking anymore. I know the answer is no. I'm just losing my sanity. Begging is all I'm capable of. And it's what he wants to hear.

I hug the pillow tight to keep from covering my butt with my hands because the burn grows in intensity with every slap he delivers. The harder he spanks, the harder I have to come. I start to buck and wriggle over his lap. "Please, Master...please, Master." I'm so close.

He stops rather abruptly. I expect him to give me a break, maybe rub my ass while I pant and catch my breath, but instead, he pulls me up to stand in front of him, between his knees.

I'm hot and discombobulated. My hair falls across my

face, and I'm close to tears. I hold my ass. Pavel tugs and rolls my nipples and puts tiny alligator clamps on one of them. I nearly come the moment he closes it. I have to shift and press my thighs together to stop. I'm more prepared for the second one.

"Master," I whimper.

Those grey eyes meet mine, and I catch the flash of approval before he hides it. He likes me this way—pleading and begging and at his mercy. Desperate to come.

He reaches around to cup my ass, pushing my hands away. He kneads it, pulling me closer, then he starts to play with the buttplug, pumping it slowly.

"Oh!" I can't control the quivers that explode in my belly. He pumps again, short fast pumps. I press my fingers over my clit as I throw back my head and come, unable to stop myself.

"I'm sorry, Master," I gasp as soon as I can catch my breath. My hands fall onto his shoulders because my legs won't hold me up.

A tear streaks down my face although I'm not even sure what it's for.

Pavel thumbs it away, studying my face. "It's okay, blossom," he murmurs. "It was an accident." He adjusts the nipple clamps, then guides me back over his knee.

This time he uses the paddle on me, and I jolt with the intensity. It's way different than his hand—much harder. And hurty. He spanks me quickly, alternating buttcheeks, right, then left.

I squirm and writhe under the spanks at first—I can't help it. But when he continues paddling, my last bit of resistance lets go. I surrender to his will, to the pain. At the same time, the upset of the audition, my stress over not telling Pavel, his disappointment in me all bubble up to the surface.

A sob breaks from my throat, and then I totally lose it.

Pavel stops immediately. "Oh, *malysh*."

~

Pavel

Tonight I want to tear out my hair when Kayla cries. It happens sometimes. She cried the first night we played—not during the scene, but after. She needed aftercare, and I didn't give it. Even though I know it's probably just an emotional release from the strain of her traumatic day, I feel like the biggest *mudak*.

I don't show my distress—that would only make her bottle her release in an effort to please me. I rub her ass with one hand and her back with the other. I don't interrupt by asking her if she's okay or what went wrong. I may not be the most experienced dom, but I know enough to make this a safe space for anything that comes out.

But as she lets out a torrent of tears, I'm sorry I promised not to kill the television director. I really, really want to pound his face right now. Or maybe it's just my own face I want to pound.

After a while, her sobs slow and then stop. I gently remove the plugs. She's still dripping wet, so I know no matter what happened emotionally, my little flower is turned on.

"Crawl up on the bed, blossom." I keep my voice soft—there's no command in my tone, only gentleness. I'm not sure if she needs to be fucked or held right now, so I'm trying to read her.

Kayla instantly obeys, crawling up farther on the bed, lying on her belly with her legs spread wide in clear invitation.

"Is that how you want it, *malysh*?" I break my own rule

and ask. I stroke and squeeze her reddened ass, making a sound of contentment in my throat.

When I rub between her legs, she makes the same sound. "Yes, Master. Please."

Another mental snapshot. So damn sweet.

I strip out of my clothes and crawl up behind her, pushing her damp blonde hair from one side of her tear-stained face to brush my lips over her temple. She arches her ass up when my cock trails between her legs.

I push in easily, her channel is soaked and swollen. I move slowly, arcing in and out with reverent glides. Filling her, reveling in the glory of everything Kayla—her tight cunt. Her punished ass. Her sweet, sweet submission.

It starts without urgency. Just pleasure. Easy strokes. The communion of two bodies. But Kayla starts crooning, "Master… Master" over and over again in that breathy, need-soaked voice, and my dick can't take it any longer. I pick up my speed, pumping into her, riding the wave. I take off her nipple clamps so the rush of blood returning to them will stimulate her orgasm, then I work a hand beneath her pelvis to rub her clit. She immediately comes.

Her climax brings on mine, and I'm lost in it. It's not rockets and fireworks this time. More like a safe space. Home. Not that my home was ever safe. But this is the way home should feel.

I lower my body onto Kayla's and kiss her neck.

She sighs contentedly. "I love you, Master."

My heart—the poor organ that's already been strained beyond recognition—bursts open at her confession. I pull out and flip her to her back, pinning her wrists beside her head, blanketing her body with mine again. "You are *fucking everything* to me," I swear fiercely. I don't know anything about love. I've never known it. But my words are the truest I've ever spoken.

Kayla strains against my hold. She wants to pull me down—maybe for a kiss, maybe because it's too intense for us to look at each other now that we've exposed ourselves to the bone, but I don't let her. I make her stare into my eyes until I'm sure she believes me.

Her eyes get bright with tears. "Please kiss me," she warbles.

I kiss the hell out of her, my mouth devouring hers, my lips an instrument I wield for war. I fuck her mouth with my tongue, and my semi-hard dick slips back home in this position for a few last glorious strokes. I kiss her until she's breathless, panting and moaning, and then I back off, roll us to our sides and pull her body against mine.

She rests her head on my biceps, her cheek on my chest. "Thank you," she murmurs.

But still I can't get over my guilt. The sense I may have done the wrong thing with someone I never want to hurt.

I don't know how long we lie together in the silence. I don't want to get up until she's been held long enough. She needs the aftercare, especially considering I broke her. Finally she stirs and moves away from me.

"I'm hungry now, Master."

I drop a kiss on the top of her head and roll off the bed to order us some food. Then I pick up my phone and return to the bed with her soft aftercare blanket, which I drape over her. I sit with my back against the wall. "I need that name, blossom."

She lifts her head and licks her lips, blinking those wide eyes at me. "It's Blake Ensign."

"Thank you." I pull her pillow close to my hip, so she can curl against my leg, and I can stroke her hair.

I text Dima, our bratva cell's hacker. *Kayla got casting couched by this douche: Blake Ensign. I need an address, so I can deal with him. Please and thank you.*

Dima texts back immediately. *On it.*

I text Maxim next because I doubt he would appreciate me texting his wife personally. *Tell Sasha I did not appreciate her advice to my girl.*

Maxim texts me back a few minutes later. *Sasha's reply: uh oh.* He sends a second message, *What's your plan with the* mudak*?*

I reply, *I'm going to hurt him.* I said before that I don't get mad, I get even, but tonight, there's a rage to my violence.

Maxim: *Good.*

"Room service." A man calls as he knocks on the door.

"Leave it outside," I snarl, even though Kayla's fully covered by the blanket. No other man's going to even think about Kayla tonight without getting my fist in his teeth.

Kayla

I wake up because Pavel's no longer in the bed. I climb out in the darkness, reaching for the soft, fuzzy blanket he wraps me in after we play and pulling it around my shoulders. I look for his shoes and wallet—or some other sign that he's left the room, but they are still here. I see three empty bottles from the mini-bar on the dresser.

I find Pavel leaning on the balcony with another tiny liquor bottle clutched in his hand.

"Master?"

"*Malysh.* I'm sorry I woke you." He doesn't move.

"No, you didn't. I mean, I missed you in the bed." I catch sight of his normally impassive face and catch a glimpse of a torture before he scrubs his hand across his neatly trimmed beard. "What's wrong?"

"Come here." He opens one arm, and I press myself

against him. His addictive scent mingles with the sharper tones of vodka.

"What is it?" I press, knowing he probably won't share on his own.

"Are you all right, Kayla?" He turns his gaze full on me like I'm the one who's just drained four bottles of liquor and is standing outside looking bereft.

"Yes. Are you?"

"I don't want to play that way with you again," he says quietly.

My heart starts beating like he's breaking up with me. But he's not. He can't be, he's holding me close against his body.

"What way?"

"Punishing you until you cry. That was wrong. I'm sorry."

"No." I press myself even closer to him, like I could meld our two bodies, so we'd never come apart again. "It wasn't wrong. I *needed* that. You gave me the release I craved. Why are you upset?"

"*Upset.*" He repeats the word with a bitter chuckle, like doms aren't allowed to be upset.

I start connecting the dots. He's told me so little, but they do connect. He told me he couldn't play at non-consent. He's always telling me I'm free to go. Somewhere in his life, he's seen something ugly.

The balcony tilts and spins. Everyone thinks this is wrong—what we do. Now even Pavel does, too.

Is it wrong? Sick?

But I can't believe that. Not with how close I feel to this man right now—even though he shares nothing of himself, he just told me I'm his everything.

He's my everything, too.

"What are you afraid of, Pavel? That you'll hurt me? That I won't use my safe word when I should?"

He turns to face me fully, and I'm struck by how much pain is in his eyes. He cradles my face in his hands. "Am I hurting you, Kayla? I mean, I did. I hurt you tonight."

"Stop," I interrupt before he goes any further down that path. "I love the way you hurt me. Why are you so worried about it? Did someone say something?" It suddenly occurs to me that my roommates may be taking their case elsewhere. To Sasha, maybe? And it got back to him?

"My father—" Pavel stops and scrubs a hand over his soft beard again.

His father. *Oh.* I'm instantly sick to my stomach.

"He was abusive?" I guess.

Pavel nods. "Yes. He nearly killed us. And finally, I killed him." Pavel stares at me, his expression awash with shame. A touch of alarm even. This is Pavel bared—the way he's never let me, or possibly anyone—see him before.

"Oh Pavel." I wrap my arms tightly around his neck, standing on tiptoe to reach.

He stands rigid for a moment, then one arm comes around me. "You're not shocked?"

"Of course, I'm shocked, Pavel. You carry a terrible burden. I'm so sorry."

He lets out a bitter laugh of disbelief. "You're sorry? For me?"

"Of course. Pavel—" I pull back enough to look him in the eye. "Did you think I'd judge you?"

He cocks his head. "Why wouldn't you?" He almost sounds suspicious, like I'm tricking him, somehow.

"Pavel, you were protecting your mother, just like you protected me at that convenience store. You did what you had to do. I love you for it."

"You love me," he repeats softly, shaking his head. "Superpower."

"What?"

"You have the capacity of...I don't know—*acceptance... presence*—that no one else has. Do you know that? You're one in a billion, little flower."

"I love you."

Pavel groans like a wounded animal and gathers me up against his body. His breath sounds ragged in my hair.

It's the third time I've said I love him tonight. Each time seems to penetrate him deeper. He hasn't made it wrong, but he hasn't said it back. After what I just learned, I can be patient. He probably hasn't known much love in his life.

I'm going to show him it's not a superpower. It's something we can both do, together.

11

Pavel

The next morning, I edge my little slave for hours with my mouth between her legs. She weeps, pounding her fists against my shoulders, begging for release. She's such a good subbie, waiting for my permission. Not that I would punish her if she did come.

Not after I broke her last night.

Even if she isn't, I'm still too raw from it. I'm starting to think there's no pain I inflict on her that I don't feel myself. Strange for a stone-cold sadist.

When I'm about to die of need myself, I put her on her knees and forearms and fuck her until she sobs. This time I don't feel bad about her tears. This is the only kind of crying I want out of her. The too-much-pleasure variety that leaves her wrung-out with bliss for hours afterward.

I wait until my climax comes on hard, then bark, "come," as I bury myself balls-deep and die a small death. Kayla's muscles squeeze around my dick, milking it for all its worth, and then I topple us both to our sides as she sobs out her breath.

When I roll her onto her back and wipe her tears from her face, she gives me a dreamy smile. "You're beautiful," I tell her.

She lets out a limp moan.

"I managed to get you into the spa today."

She blinks, obviously trying to come back to reality. Her hair is spread in a golden halo around her head, her face flushed a pretty shade of pink.

"Your first appointment is at one. I need to take care of some business, but I'll come back as soon as I can."

Her lips part. "Oh."

"Yes, Master," I prompt to head off the line of questioning I sense is about to start up.

"Yes, Master. Thank you, Master."

"I'm going to take a quick shower before I go." I swear to Christ I'm not the kind of guy who talks just to hear himself talk, but Kayla's vulnerability, especially after a scene, forces me to communicate far more.

"Me too," she murmurs and sits up.

I take her hand to help her off the bed and lead her into the bathroom where I wash her from head to toe. My soft, pliant slave-doll, who I will avenge like a fucking nightmare today.

I texted Dima when I woke up this morning asking for Ensign's address, he replied, *Wait until noon. Nikolai, Oleg and I are flying out to lend a hand. I'll text when we land.*

I stared at my phone for a moment, trying to identify the unfamiliar feeling swirling in my chest. Gratitude. I knew my bratva brothers had my back in business, but this thing with Kayla has nothing to do with them. Nothing at all. They've never even met her, and yet three of them dropped everything to back me up on this.

Maybe it was just that it came on the heels of Kayla's unbelievable acceptance of my patricide, but I've never felt so… open. My armor got knocked off last night, and it feels like I don't even need it.

I send Kayla out of the shower, so I can wash myself. When I come out, she's naked in the room, holding my phone. "Dima says they're outside?" She turns the screen around to face me.

Well, fuck.

"Should you be reading my texts, slave?"

She's unfazed by my stern tone. "No, sir. Why are they here? Can I meet them?"

"I told you, we have some business to take care of."

She folds her fingers underneath her chin and bats her eyelashes. "Please? I've been dying to meet your housemates. Who's here? Both twins?"

I don't know how the fuck she even knows I live with twins. Oh yeah—Sasha, of course. Really, what I didn't know was that she had any interest in my housemates at all.

"Yes, the twins. And Oleg." Gah. I run a hand through my hair. There's no harm in her meeting them, I guess. I don't know why it makes me break into a sweat. I liked keeping Kayla to myself, I guess. Keeping our relationship in the dark. In a hotel room. Where the outside world can't find us or affect us.

But it seems Kayla craves something different.

"You have ninety seconds to get dressed," I tell her, mostly to watch her scurry around while I pull on a pair of black jeans and a dark t-shirt. Wouldn't want to get blood stains on lighter clothes.

She's ready before I am, dragging a brush through her hair quickly as I open the door.

"Just for a minute. To meet them. We're not hanging out."

"Okay," she says brightly.

Something shifts in my chest. This girl.

I take her downstairs and outside where I spot a white passenger van with familiar plumbing magnets on the doors. "Over here." I take her hand, and we walk across the street.

Nikolai climbs out of the driver's side when we approach. "Wait...is she coming?"

"No, you dumb fuck," I tell him as I reach out to shake his hand and thump his shoulder. It's a rare show of appreciation on my part, and Nikolai recognizes it by thumping me back.

The other two guys pile out of the van.

"Kayla wanted to meet you guys." I rest my hand on her lower back. "This is Nikolai."

"Nikolai! Great to meet you." She throws her arms around his neck.

"Don't touch him," I growl.

"Sorry, I'm a hugger." She releases Nikolai and goes for Dima. "You must be Dima!" Another hug. This is Kayla in normal company. An adorable, friendly girl from Wisconsin who hugs people she's never met before.

It's so far from my world I feel like I stepped into a colorful rom-com movie instead of the darkness and shadows that make up my life.

"Seriously," I mutter, grinding my teeth. "Do you want me to have to kill my own brothers? Don't touch him."

Kayla forgets to be my obedient slave. She ignores me completely.

"So this is what Pavel's like in love," Dima deadpans as he accepts my handshake and shoulder clasp. "Even meaner than he was alone."

"Yeah, love doesn't look good on you, bro," Nikolai agrees.

Kayla even gets a hug out of Oleg, our giant, silent enforcer.

Un-fucking-believable.

"That's Oleg," I explain as the big guy bends down and gives her a half-hug with one giant meaty arm. "He doesn't talk." A month ago he probably wouldn't have moved, but he has his girlfriend Story now, and she has changed him completely. Where his silence was like a weapon before, now he attempts to communicate more. We're learning sign language, and he's joining conversations. He gives her the sign language salute now, which means *hello*.

"I guessed as much. I used to live with Sasha," she explains, even though they knew that. "And Pavel's not mean." She returns safely to my side, and I unclench my fists.

"Agree to disagree," Nikolai quips.

"All right," I say, tugging her backwards. "Let's get you back to the hotel."

"Can you guys stay for dinner?" Kayla asks brightly.

"No," I snap. "They can't. They're heading back to Chicago. Say goodbye."

Kayla lifts a hand and waves. "Bye guys. Nice to meet you."

I walk Kayla back across the street and through the front doors of the Four Seasons. "Be good. Enjoy the spa."

A furrow creases between her brows. "Are you guys going to—"

I stop her with a finger on her lips. "Go upstairs, *malysh*. I'll see you when I get back."

She hesitates a moment, like she's going to argue, so I raise my brows. "Yes, sir." She lifts her face for a kiss. I brush my lips over hers. The darkness of what I'm about to do already shrouds me, makes me want to keep my distance from her. To not sully her brightness with what I am.

I should let her go, I tell myself for the hundredth time.

Never, a new voice answers. A dark voice. The one that wants to consume all that Kayla is. Claim her and keep her forever. Suck everything out of her until she's dry.

Never.

What can I say? It feels right to be so wrong.

12

Pavel

"All security cameras have been put on loop and the locks are open," Dima says, his fingers clicking over the keys on his laptop in the back of the van.

Nikolai puts the van in drive and coasts forward the remaining half block until we reach the iron gates that close the entrance to Blake Ensign's home.

"The gate is...now open." Dima reports just before the gates swing wide to let us in. "I brought masks. They're in that bag." Dima doesn't look away from his screen; his fingers still move across the keyboard, clicking away. I have yet to see anything the guy can't hack with enough time.

I open the bag and stare at the ski masks. Part of me doesn't want to wear one. I want this fucker to see my face when we're talking. But I can always take it off. I pull mine out and toss out the rest to the guys.

"He lives alone?" I ask Dima.

"Yep. How else would he get blowies from all the women he casts?"

My lip curls, and Dima shoots me a look over the top

of his laptop before he snaps the lid closed. "He definitely picked the wrong actress this time."

He did. "I promised Kayla I wouldn't kill him," I warn my brothers. "So don't let me take it too far."

"We've got your back," Nikolai promises, turning from the front seat and pulling on his knit mask.

Dima taps the lid of his computer. "I have ways to hurt him that don't even require bloodshed." He pulls on his as well.

Oleg already wears his, his size and silence making him the most terrifying in appearance of the four of us.

"*Brat'ya*," I address my brothers in Russian, "*Spasibo*." Thank you.

"Wouldn't miss it for the fucking world," Nikolai says easily, sliding out of the van. "Let's do this thing."

I palm the revolver I found in the bag with the caps. Nikolai also pulls one out. Oleg prefers to rely on his hands, which are capable of snapping a man's neck with a single twitch. Dima brings the laptop along. I can't fucking wait to hear what damage he holds in there.

I do the polite thing and ring the bell. I hope to fuck he doesn't have servants in the house at the moment—scaring the innocent isn't my thing.

A mid-fifties asshole with salt and pepper hair pulls the door open, then tries to slam it shut when he catches sight of us. Oleg catches the door and shoves it in.

I point my gun in the center of Ensign's forehead. "Hey asshole. I have a few things to say to you."

"What the fuck is this?" He's not scared yet, he's pissed. The man wears entitlement like it's a second skin.

Oleg grips his throat and lifts, using his superior height to lift the bastard off his heels.

He chokes, his face turning purple, eyes bulging. Oleg

knows exactly how long to hold him. Long enough he starts thinking he might die right here in his entryway.

When he releases him, Ensign collapses in a heap on the floor. Nikolai kicks the door shut behind us.

"What—" Ensign coughs and sputters, holding his throat with one hand as he drags himself back up to his feet.

"Should we take him somewhere?" Dima affects a bored tone. "Is there a nice rug we could ruin with his blood?"

"Wh-who are you guys? What the fuck are you doing in my house?"

"Adjust his tone." I make my voice as cool and bored as Dima's but don't quite succeed. I sound invested in his pain. I *am* invested in his pain.

Oleg delivers a couple choice blows—one to his gut, one to his jaw, knocking him backward onto his ass again.

"We'll take him to the casting room. I want to see the couch where he takes his dick out." I deliver a sharp kick to his ribs. "Where is that?"

"What?" He's still more angry than scared. His face contorts with belligerence.

I point my gun right at his crotch. "You wanna keep those balls? Take me to the fucking room where you asked my girl to suck your dick."

I see a flash of fear now. He understands why we're here. What we want. Or maybe he just sees that I'm a ruthless bastard. He hides it quickly. I'll give him that—the guy's not a total coward. I actually thought he'd be softer. The kind who begged the moment he saw a gun.

"Just shoot it off," Nikolai suggests when he doesn't answer immediately.

"Upstairs." His attitude adjusts quickly. He points toward a spiral staircase. "In my office."

I kick him again. "Take us there."

He groans as he climbs to his feet. I press the tip of my revolver to the back of his head as he hobbles forward up the stairs.

"Who are you?" he asks when we get into his office. "Which girl?"

"*Which girl*," Nikolai repeats the damning phrase. "How many have there been?"

He doesn't answer.

"How many yesterday?" I ask, just before Oleg delivers a blow to his jaw that sends him careening into the heavy maple desk.

Dima takes a seat and cracks open the laptop. "Looks like you saw forty-five women yesterday, is that right?"

Ensign shoots him a frightened glance, like that kind of information wasn't public knowledge.

"Yes, I am in your email, in case you were wondering. I'm also in your bank account. The one at Wells Fargo, the one at Fidelity, the one at Vanguard, and also the off-shore account in Barbados. Looks like your current balance is two million, eight hundred fifty thousand and some change. Does that sound right?"

Ensign pales, shooting scared glances between me and Dima. "Wh-what the fuck is going on here?"

Oleg punches him in the gut.

I fold my arms across my chest. Honestly, I'm afraid if I do get my hands on him, I'll finish the job. "I thought I made it pretty clear. You asked my girl to suck your dick. I'm going to kick your ass. I'm also thinking about cutting your dick off to prevent future incidents. We'll see how long it takes you to say sorry."

"I'm sorry!" He holds his hands up and shoots another glance at Dima. "Wh-what is he doing with my money?"

"Looks like he's more worried about his money than his dick," I observe. "You set up to drain him?"

"With the click of a button," Dima confirms. "Which one do I start with?"

"How much is in the Vanguard account?" I ask.

"That's his smallest. Two hundred eighty thousand."

"Wait, wait, wait, wait, wait! I'm sorry about your girlfriend. Who is she? I'll give her the part. I'll make her a star.

I hesitate then send my knuckles into his nose, breaking it. "You think I'd let her anywhere near you?"

He groans, holding his gushing nose. "I'll get her a part with the studio—on another show. I can do that."

"You can do that." I make my voice sound withering, but I glance at Nikolai to see his take on it.

He shrugs like the solution is worth considering.

"I can do it." Ensign's talking fast. "Lots of parts are being cast right now for next season. I could get her a part on *Bank Bandits* or *Bad Boys*. An on-going role. If she's any good, it would open doors for her."

"If they're not your shows, how can you get her the part?"

"I'll talk to the casting director." Ensign holds his gushing nose. "I can say she's a friend—or, or my niece—and I need this as a favor. I guarantee I can get her something."

Gospodi. I want to help Kayla this way. But what if he's just trying to get her name to nail me?

I look at Dima. "Take the money from his Vanguard accounts." Dima hesitates a moment because it was a bluff. I was supposed to know it was a bluff. And now I'm asking my cell brother to commit another felony for me.

"You have forty-eight hours to make it happen. If you do, I'll put the money back."

Dima clicks the button. "Account drained."

"I'll do it!" Ensign agrees. "What's her name?"

"Kayla Winstead. And if that girl does not get treated like fucking gold, I'm coming back for another visit." I bring the butt of the gun to his forehead again. "She doesn't know you got her the job. Understand?"

"Understood," he croaks.

"You come looking for me, you're a dead man. Forty-eight hours."

"I'll take care of it." He reaches for tissues on the desk and uses a wad of them to hold up to his nose. "And you'll put my money back."

"That's the arrangement. If you don't come through, we'll empty the rest of them."

"No." He slices his hand through the air. "It's done."

"Good." I glance at Oleg who nods and punches Ensign hard enough to knock him out.

The four of us walk out the door and climb in the van. "Honestly, I was hoping he'd be harder to break," Nikolai says as he backs the van quickly down the drive. Dima makes the gate open with his laptop, and we're out.

"Same," I agree. "You think he's good for it?" I ask.

"Yeah, I do. Here's my guess," Nikolai says. "I'd bet this isn't the first time he's had to offer that solution. There's probably been threatened lawsuits before."

"Fucker," I mutter. "Kayla can't know about this. Make sure you don't say anything in front of Sasha, those two don't keep many secrets."

"When do we ever talk business in front of Sasha?" Dima scoffs.

"I know. Of course you wouldn't. I'm just making sure."

"You did the right thing." Nikolai guesses at my misgivings.

I sure as fuck hope so. If anything I did ever hurt Kayla, I'd never forgive myself.

~

Kayla

Lara calls when I get back from the spa. At first,I just stare at my phone, not sure I want to answer. Not sure whether I'm going to tell her what happened.

But after spending two and a half hours having my feet massaged, my nails painted and my face peeled and moisturized, I've come to a realization: Pavel takes care of me.

He takes care of me like no one in my life ever has—and I had a nice, wholesome upbringing with two parents who drove me to every rehearsal and never missed a single performance.

So I'm going to surrender control and let Pavel take care of Blake Ensign and forget about my good-girl misgivings over what he's doing.

"Hi Lara."

"I just wanted to check to see how the audition went yesterday." she asks.

I appreciate the check-in, even if it's a day late. "Um, not great. But that's okay. I'm chalking it up to experience. At least I made call-backs."

I wish to hell Blake Ensign hadn't ruined that high point for me. For a minute there, I'd been damn proud of myself. Of my success. Of actually doing the thing I came here to do. I'd gone into that first audition as an empty vessel, and I'd filled it with the part I was supposed to play. I'd moved them, just as Pavel had promised.

The fact that I got a call-back proves it.

I shouldn't let a first class asshole like Blake Ensign diminish that little win.

If I did it once, I can do it again. Now I know what it takes. Stripping myself bare. Dropping all pretentions. Just *being*. All the things Pavel has demanded from me. I've been worried that he was distracting me from my career, when, in fact, he was the ticket.

"Oh." Lara sounds disappointed. "All right, hon. We'll get you another one. I've gotta go. Have a good rest of your weekend."

"You too," I singsong, even though I know she's already hanging up.

Crawling onto the bed, I open the reading app on my phone and find a romance novel to read—a sexy werewolf one because I love me an alpha male, but Pavel walks in before I even start it.

"Master!" I scramble up off the bed and throw myself at him.

He bands his arm around my back and lets me smash myself against his body. "That's… sweet." He sounds surprised. I guess I haven't greeted him this way before. His body is a tense rock against mine, like he's bracing himself. Or holding himself back.

"Thank you for the spa day. It was so nice."

He fists my hair and pulls my head back. "I want to do bad things to you." I guess he's already over his misgivings about hurting me.

"Did you… um… were you visiting Blake Ensign?"

"I took care of it." There's a finality to his tone, but I still push.

"What did you do?"

He disengages himself from me and steps into the bathroom without answering. I hear the sound of him washing his hands. I follow him in. He rubs a washcloth over a dark spot on his hunter green shirt, and I see the remainder of blood there.

"You said we don't lie to each other," I accuse.

Pavel turns and raises his brows, pinning me with a sharp look. "I won't lie to you, Blossom. I will also never make you an accessory to a crime. My job is to protect you. That's what I will do."

My breath leaves me in a whoosh. Like every time he reveals this side of him I'm simultaneously shocked and turned on. Afraid and swoony.

I move forward and insinuate myself into his arms again. "I like what you do," I murmur.

Pavel lets out an exhale. His body relaxes a few degrees, and he kisses the top of my head. "Clothes off, little slave. I need to be inside you."

13

Kayla

I hate Sunday nights after Pavel leaves when every inch of my body still feels him, yet he's hundreds of miles away. My heart gets on the plane with him, abandons me and leaves me with a gaping hole in my chest.

Monday mornings are even worse. Every weekend feels harder than the last, and the fact that now I feel like I can't talk to my roommates about it makes it even worse.

It's a form of sub-drop. The endorphins from the high of the weekend with Pavel wearing off and leaving me blue. Not like the burst into tears kind I hate but low nonetheless.

I force myself into the shower, recalling every moment of the weekend—good and bad.

When I get out, my phone rings. I pick it up and swipe across the screen when I see it's Lara.

"Hi, Lara, what's up?"

"Well, I'm not sure. The casting agent from Black Diamond studios called—you didn't get the part." She adds the last bit quickly, like she didn't want me to get my hopes up even for a second. "But she would like you to come back in to audition for the next season of *Bad Boys*."

"Really?"

"Yes. I guess she really liked you. Sounds like maybe she's in your corner now."

My optimistic spark flares to life, and I start feeling more like myself. "That's amazing. Oh my God, I'm so happy. So when's the audition?"

"Well, it sounded informal—I don't think there is an actual audition. She wanted you to come down to the studio to read lines for the part. Kayla, I don't want to jinx this, but it sounds like you're on the short-list for this part!"

"What's the part? Do you know?"

"No. I don't think it's a lead role, but regardless, it would be a great opportunity."

"Of course, it would! I'm thrilled. When do they want me?"

"Today. She said anytime between noon and three. You just show up at Black Diamond and ask to see Claire Peacock. She's the casting director."

"Great! I'll get ready now." I run to my closet and start frantically throwing clothes out on the bed.

"What time should I tell her?"

"Um…" I try to put on a pair of panties one-headed while I hold the phone. "Twelve-thirty. I don't want to look too eager. Or do I?"

Lara gives a throaty laugh. "Twelve-thirty sounds good. I'll give her the message. Call me when it's over to let me know how it went."

"Will do."

I hang up, a goofy grin stretching across my face. Lara doesn't usually ask for a report on how things went, so that must be a sign that she has high hopes for me. For this.

"Oh my God, you guys!" I run out of my room in

nothing but my black panties, looking for my housemates. "I got another call-back!"

"Whoop whoop!" Kimberly calls from the kitchen. "You did something right."

The sickening memory of Ensign's office tries to crowd into my brain and dampen my enthusiasm, but I shove it away. I did something right at the first audition, and that's why I got this call-back. Ensign's an ass who doesn't know good talent, and fortunately, he had nothing to do with this.

"Yep. I didn't even have to suck anyone's dick," I say, trying to make light of it. My words choke me a little, though, and Kimberly cocks her head.

I didn't tell them about what happened. How could I? They'd want me to hashtag me-too it, but I don't want to be famous for being sexually harassed. I want to be famous based on my skill.

Besides, I didn't think I could talk about it without spilling Pavel's reaction to it. What he did. I'm still alternating between being queasy and weak-kneed over it. Pavel's a bad boy, no doubt about it, but that's the attraction. He gives me his undivided attention. His protection. His possessive dominance.

He's a fantasy dom. After living in Los Angeles for five years trying to get discovered, to catch someone's eye and finding I'm just another petite blonde in a whole sea of them, Pavel's attention heals me.

He makes me feel special when I'd started to think I was nothing. He makes me feel beautiful. Hot. Alluring. He takes care of me.

And yes, he's leaving for Russia. He lives in another city. So I know it can't go on, that he's not going to stick, but I'm falling hard for him, anyway.

"Well, when's your call-back?" Kimberly asks.

"Today! Twelve-thirty. Come help me pick out an outfit?"

"Wear your turquoise blouse with the open shoulders—it brings out your eyes."

I run back to my room. "With what pants?" I shout from there.

"Black pencil-legs. And your high-heeled black boots. You're going to rock this."

I *am* going to rock this. I throw on the outfit Kimberly suggested and start blow-drying my hair. I'm already picturing the phone calls I'll make if I actually land a part. The first one will be to my mom. Her cheerleading is the reason I'm still in Los Angeles trying to make it happen.

In my scenario, Pavel would already know. He would know because he's been with me every step of the way. I pick up the phone to text him. *I got another call-back at the studio. Don't worry, not the same director.*

The phone rings immediately.

"Hi." I'm instantly shy. That's what this man does to me. He makes my heart pound every time we talk. It's like a shot of adrenaline straight to my arm. I should have called him this morning when I felt down, but I didn't want to be a clingy mess. Now I have something to share.

"Little slave." Pavel's voice is gravelly and soft. I picture him, heavy-lidded and hungry for me.

"I'm going back in to read lines at twelve-thirty—for a different show."

"They're going to love you."

"I think this is all because—Pavel, you helped me."

He stays quiet, so I go on.

"When I went to that first audition, I was scared that I wasn't confident enough and didn't know who or how to be. When you told me to just go in open like that—well, I think it made a difference. That's why this casting director keeps calling me back."

"There's no human being on the planet who wouldn't feel your magnetism. You are a natural. Go be that again."

"I wish I had you here to open me back up again." I lower my voice, leaning into one hip, projecting myself through the phone, all the way to Chicago.

"Where are you?"

"In my bathroom, putting on makeup."

"Wash your hands."

A little thrill runs through me at the simple command. The signal that Pavel's taking the reins, even from a distance.

I turn on the water and obey. "Okay."

"Now I want you to lean your back against the wall and close your eyes."

I totter backward on my heels until my ass hits the door. "Okay." My voice is breathy. Excited.

"Slide your fingers into your panties. Are you wearing panties?"

"Yes. Black panties."

"Good. Put your fingers inside those panties and tap your clit for me." I tap the pad of my index finger over my clit again and again.

Pavel waits, so I don't stop. Quivers start to move through me and heat blooms.

"Now circle it. Feather-light touch."

"Oh." I suck my lower lip into my mouth as I barely trace a light circle around my clit. "Mmm." Another tremor makes my knees give out.

"Rub a little harder. Make it good, little slave, or the next time I'm there, I will spend all night punishing you. That's my pussy you're touching right now, and I want it touched right."

"Oh my God," I breathe, my fingers quickening.

"I will whip those pretty breasts with the new flogger I bought you. And then your belly. Your inner thighs. Your back. And finally your ass. I will turn your ass red-hot, and then I will lube it up and fuck it until your pussy weeps. And I won't let you come, little slave."

"N-now?" I gasp.

Thankfully Pavel understands. "Come right now." He makes the command sharp, like I might disobey, and I go off. I plunge two fingers in my channel just to feel my walls squeeze while I use the heel of my hand to press and rub my clit.

"Ohhhh-*oh*. Wow." I sigh.

"You've got me harder than stone here, blossom. And I don't have that hot, wet perfect mouth of yours to take care of me."

"S-sorry, Master." My limbs feel like liquid gold is coursing through them, blissful relaxation soaking through my entire body.

"Now, *malysh*, you go to that studio and show them this. Beautiful, beautiful you. And they will scramble to find the part that is perfect for you."

"Thank you, Master," I whisper. I feel wonderful again. "I love you."

"I love you, Kayla," he murmurs back, and the hugest smile beams back at me from the mirror. "Break a leg."

"Thank you. Love you. Goodbye."

I end the call feeling like the flower Pavel sees me as. Opened by him. Nearing full-bloom.

14

Pavel

I hear from Kayla Wednesday that she got a part on a series Ensign named. Her joy almost made it worth living with the knowledge that Ensign was still breathing. I had Dima transfer Ensign's money back to his account although I considered making him sweat for a few more days.

I sent Kayla three dozen multi-colored roses to congratulate her, but the need to tell her in person made me stupid. I'm already on thin ice around here, but I asked Ravil if I could leave early for the weekend, and he flat-out refused.

"Make your choice," he said.

No one's going to hand you the life you want. You have to take it.

So I choose.

I fucking choose Kayla. If Ravil wants to kill me for it, he will. But I don't believe that's what he has in store for me. He's showing me how to control my own destiny, the way he controlled his, even while under Igor's heel.

I knock on Maxim and Sasha's door Thursday noon.

"You done making Sasha scream yet?" I ask when Maxim comes to the door with his shirt off and hair tousled.

"Don't talk about my wife unless you want to die," he returns easily. "What do you want?"

"To buy you both lunch."

"Oh, damn. I sense a pitch coming."

Yes, I am that douche.

"Pavel's pitching?" Sasha calls out. "Ooh—I can't wait to hear it. Do I get to come?"

"I believe you just did," Maxim brags. "Several times, on my tongue."

"I did *not* consent to hear that." I put my fingers up to my eyes like blinders.

"Of course you get to come, it's your money, *caxapok*."

"Which you control," she pouts, appearing behind Maxim in a silky purple bathrobe, her red hair in a wild tangled mess from their love-making.

"We'll be out in thirty," Maxim promises.

"Yeah?" Frankly, I can't believe he didn't already shut me down. The fact that he's even entertaining my pitch gives me hope.

Maxim smirks as he shuts the door. "Sure. You never pay for lunch."

I find my own lips lifting a little. Maybe this all could work.

Sasha and Maxim emerge in twenty minutes. Sasha's wearing a bustier over a long-sleeved sheer top, showing off her brick house body, as usual. Maxim allows it because it brings Sasha joy. Exuberance for life is her personality, but I'm sure he'd like to kill every man who looks, myself included. Obviously, I take pains not to ever look.

"There he is," Sasha says as she breezes past the kitchen and catches my arm. "I can't wait to hear the whole scoop."

"Don't touch him," Maxim minces through gritted teeth, and Sasha flashes a wide grin before she behaves and drops my arm. Maxim, our fixer, somehow managed to tame his rebellious bride but just barely.

We pull on our jackets. "Where are we going?" Sasha asks.

"You pick," I tell her.

"Let's walk to that new gyro place. I'm starving." She throws the door open and breezes into the elevator.

"Cheap date," I mutter as Maxim and I follow. "I like it."

"She's not your date," Maxim growls.

"Poor choice of words," I agree.

"So what did you do to the director?" Sasha purrs when we're inside the elevator heading to the ground floor.

"Don't ask him that," Maxim warns, not that I would tell.

"I heard she got a part." Sasha lifts her brows and a ripple of warning makes the hair at the back of my neck stand. If Sasha put it together, how long before Kayla does?

My heart inexplicably speeds up like I'm in danger. Maybe I am. Danger of toppling this card house I'm trying to construct with Kayla.

Somehow, Sasha reads my alarm. "Ah, so you *were* responsible. I figured. She doesn't know," she assures me. "She thinks she got it on her own. You'd better make sure it stays that way."

"*You'd* better—" I start, then modify my tone when Maxim's nostril's flare. I pinch the bridge of my nose. "Please don't tell her."

"Aw, Pavel said *please*." Sasha flicks a delighted look Maxim's way. "Love is changing him."

I want to deny I'm in love, but I stop myself because it

would be a lie. I *am* in love. That's the whole point of this lunch. I'm in love, and I'm trying to figure out how to make a life with the girl that stitched the shreds of my soul back together.

The elevator stops on the ground floor, and we get out and walk past Maykl, a bratva brigadier, who serves as a doorman for the building. A very well-armed and protective doorman.

"Sasha?" I try not to say it in a growl.

Maykl jogs to open the door for her.

"I won't tell her," she promises, giving Maykl an entitled smile and wave as she passes through. "She'd be devastated. She thinks she made it on talent, just like she always dreamed."

"Thanks, man," I mutter to Maykl as he holds it for me, too. I try to push away the gnawing sense that I fucked up. "She *has* made it on talent," I insist when we're out on the street.

"Right. I know," Sasha says quickly. "Kayla's talented, for sure." I hear the lack of conviction in her voice and want to strangle her. She's an actress, too, and she modified her dreams because of her forced marriage to Maxim. Things have worked out for her here, though. She got the leading role in the *Anna Karenina* musical recently.

I would never ask that of Kayla, though. Her heart is set on making it big.

The sun is out, but the April wind whips off the lake and through us as we walk the few city blocks to the gyro joint. Maxim and Sasha order first, then I place my order and pay and join them at a table.

"So?" Sasha rubs her hands together like she's excited. She's making it easy on me, and I'm humbled by the fact that they're even here listening to me.

I look from one to the other. "Real estate in Los Angeles seems like it's always a safe bet," I begin.

Maxim flicks his brows—whether that means he's in agreement or surprised by the topic, I'm not sure.

"I've been doing some research, and the median cost of a home in Los Angeles is 950 grand. The prices have trended upward at a rate of 11.8 percent year-over-year. I believe that means a large number of residents have to rent. Investing in a small but upscale apartment building could prove lucrative as a long-term investment. I called about one when I was there—twelve units plus a penthouse suite for five million, three. There's a pool on the roof." I take a long, desperate sip of the Dr. Pepper I ordered. My mouth is so damn dry.

"What do you propose?" Maxim asks.

"I have eighty-seven grand saved. That's not even close to ten percent, but I wondered if you'd either consider financing my mortgage, or becoming an outright business partner with me."

A server brings our gyros to the table, and we dig in.

"You'd manage the property?" Maxim wants to know.

"Yes." It's not completely out of my wheelhouse. I've seen how Ravil manages his properties and lent force or muscle or whatever he required when he required it.

"Full-time? On-site?"

I keep myself from flinching at the question. "That's my idea."

"Have you talked to Ravil?"

"Indirectly. He told me he won't let me out. But then he said no one's going to hand me the life I want—I have to take it. So this is me taking it."

Maxim's lips twitch. "Sounds like you could be on the right path."

A whisper of relief blows over me.

"So?" I look between the two of them.

Maxim turns to look at Sasha.

"Yes!" she exclaims, clapping her hands. "I'm so happy for you."

Maxim watches his wife with amusement. To me, he says, "You know it's all contingent on you keeping Kayla happy, right? Because that's clearly all Sasha cares about."

I swallow. Not because I don't *want* to keep Kayla happy. But because there's never been a job I've been less qualified for. I have the emotional range of an icicle. I've never had a girlfriend. I know how to satisfy her sexually, yes. But other than that, I know nothing about keeping a woman. But I nod because that's what this means. That's why I need to be in L.A.

Maxim finishes his gyro and wipes his lips with a napkin. "I'll work on terms."

I barely stop the sputter of surprised relief coming from my mouth. "That's it? You're in? That easy?"

Maxim smirks. "You haven't seen my terms, yet."

"Right."

"Or Ravil's," he adds. "You won't walk free, I know that much. He may want a taste of this venture. Or for you to set up another one on his behalf."

"Of course. He's the *pakhan.*" I wouldn't chafe against any terms Ravil set up for me. Maxim's a different story, but at the moment, I'm inclined to feel nothing but gratitude.

This past week my brothers have shown me they are brothers in the truest sense. Not just in bratva business but beyond. It's more than I ever believed possible.

"Does Kayla know?" Sasha asks.

I shake my head. "Don't say anything. Not until I've worked out the details. —Please," I add.

Sasha finishes her gyro and crumples up the paper it

came wrapped in. "I won't. And Maxim is right. This all hinges on her happiness. You fuck her over, and I'll bury you. Understand?" She picks up a plastic fork and points it at my throat.

I'm feeling so light, I actually smile as I snatch it from her hand. "I will *never* fuck her over."

Hurting her is another issue.

It's something I do on a regular basis, on purpose and on accident.

That's the thing that terrifies me the most.

Kayla

I hold the plastic keycard up to the hotel room door and push it open when the lock lights up in green. As soon as I'm inside, I follow orders and call Pavel.

It's Saturday afternoon and Pavel isn't here yet because his boss wouldn't let him come yesterday—I guess he had a job to do. I don't know—I didn't ask, of course. Business is off-limits. He called me this afternoon to tell me he was getting on a plane, and I needed to come to the Four Seasons and check in for him.

"I don't want you waiting in that lobby turning all the men on every time you cross and uncross your hot-as-fuck legs," he told me. "And I don't want you carrying your own bag in. Let the bellhop do it. You get your glass of champagne, get in the room and call me when you're there. Hopefully I'll be off the plane by then."

He picks up now. "Are you there?"

"I'm here, Master."

"Strip." It sounds like he's in a car. Oh God, I hope he didn't Uber here and a driver can overhear.

"Are-are you here?"

"I said strip, little slave. The only answer should be *yes, Master.*"

Excitement flutters in my stomach at his dommy tone. I don't know why I love to be bossed around so much. Maybe I do need therapy, but at this moment, I don't care. I'm desperate to be with Pavel again. To have him in charge of me, controlling me, making me submit.

Not that he ever has to make me. I'm not the kind of submissive who requires taming. I'm a service submissive, always trying to please.

"Yes, Master."

"Good girl."

"Um, are you staying on the phone?"

"Yes. Put me on speaker while you take off your clothes."

I obey, dropping the phone on the bed as I shimmy out of the body-hugging sweater dress I'd put on. "All of them?" I ask. I sound breathless.

"Are you wearing heels?"

"High heeled boots."

He groans. "I'm biting my knuckle, little slave. But take them off. You can put it all back on when I'm done with you. I'll need you to show me the sexy outfit you picked for me."

"Yes, Master." I unzip my boots and pull them off, then strip out of my red panties and bra. "I'm naked, sir."

"Lie down on the bed, blossom."

I crawl up on the bed. "Face up or face down, Master?"

"Face… which way do you lie when you touch yourself at home, little slave?"

"Face down."

"Fuck. Me."

I laugh a little. It's not like Pavel to express his torture.

He so seldom shows his cards. Could it be that he's starting to warm up? To open up?

"I want you to lie face down, blossom. Use a pillow if you need it. And I want those fingers between your legs."

"Yes, Master." I slide a pillow under my chest and my fingers between my legs.

"Tell me what you feel."

"I'm already wet, Master," I confess. A few weeks ago, I wouldn't have been able to answer him, but he's made so many demands of me during our phone sex that I've lost some of my inhibitions. I wouldn't say I can dirty-talk now, but I can at least respond to his questions.

"Good girl. I need you to keep yourself wet for me but *do not come.*"

"Yes, Master."

"You keep that phone on, so I can hear you. If you come before I get there, I will whip you with my belt and leave that pretty pussy empty while I fuck your ass, do you understand?"

I whimper because the threat almost makes me come.

"*Do you understand?*"

"Y-yes, sir. Yes, I understand."

"Tell me what you're doing."

"Um, I'm rubbing my clit with my middle finger, sir."

I hear a low rumble of approval. Again, that's new.

"Good. You get that pussy ready for me because I'm going to need to be inside you the second I get in that room."

I whimper again.

"*Do not come.*"

"I won't," I say quickly. "I'll be good, Master."

"I missed you yesterday, little flower. I'm sorry I couldn't be there to take care of your needs."

"I… I missed you, too." It's hard to talk with how

turned on I am. Heat swirls in my pelvis, my swelling clit throbs. My slick folds are soaked and plump, greedy for my touch.

No, greedy for *his* touch.

"Please," I murmur.

"*No.*" His voice is sharp. "Do not make yourself come."

"I won't. I need you," I moan.

I hear the screech of brakes and then the slam of a door. "That pussy belongs to me, blossom. I will be very disappointed if you disobey me this time. I mean it."

I let out a little cry and pull my hand out from underneath me. "I won't!"

"Did you stop touching yourself?"

"How do you do that?" I ask, in wonder.

He lets out a soft chuckle. I hear the ding of an elevator. Thank God. He's close.

"I told you to touch yourself, and that's what I want you to do."

I moan. "Yes, sir." I slide my hand between my legs.

Another ding of the elevator, but this time I hear it both through the phone and down the hall.

"Open the door for me." His command is even softer —a habit he has. The more intense things get, the softer he goes.

I leap from the bed and throw the door open.

His lips slam down on mine the moment he comes through it. It's a punishing kiss, his tongue lashing between my lips. He slants his head one way, then the other, then back to the first direction.

He walks me backward to the bed, capturing my wrists in his hands. He lifts them over my head, bending to suck one nipple.

"Please!" I cry out. I'm already so desperate to come.

"No." He sounds so firm it's almost angry, but I know by the prodding of his thick erection against my belly that he's in as much pain as I am right now.

He sucks my other nipple into his mouth, scraping his teeth over the sensitive flesh.

"P-please. Pavel!"

His lids droop. "*Master.*"

"Master!"

He kisses me again, still holding my wrists high above my head. "I love it when you beg, sweet flower. Take my cock out." He frees my hands and goes to work on my nipples, squeezing and rolling them between his fingertips.

I work the buckle on his belt, my fingers shaking. Opening it, I unbutton his trousers and lower the zipper. His cock bulges through the gap, straining to be free. I push his boxer briefs down to wrap my hand around it. "Master, may I please suck your cock?"

I revel in the shudder that runs through him. The surge of his cock in my hand.

"Wet it." The command is gravelly and deep.

I drop to my knees, gripping the root of his cock. Licking my lips to moisten them, I stroke his cock from root to tip then slide his mushroom head into my mouth. I take him in slowly, tasting a drop of his salty essence as I swirl my tongue on the underside of his length.

He weaves his fingers into my hair, more a caress than domination, but then his words rasp out harshly. *"That's enough."*

I pop off immediately, my gaze flying to his face to see if I displeased him.

The hunger I see there makes my heart pound. He's starting to show himself to me. That, more than anything he's ever done, thrills me the most.

"Show me how you touched yourself before I came in."

I stand, my fingers curling between my legs, but he shakes his head and lifts his chin toward the bed.

"I-I was like this, Master." I crawl up on the mattress and lie flat on my belly, my hand under my hips. Knowing he's watching makes it a different game. I part my legs wider to give him a view, arch my ass in the air.

I'm impossibly wet, dying to have him inside me.

"That's pretty. *Gospodi*, that's fucking beautiful, Kayla." He climbs over me. "I spend every weekend memorizing how *fucking gorgeous* you look when you're obeying your master."

My body hums everywhere with the thrill of his praise. I hump my hand, showing him how much it turns me on to please him. To have him watching me.

I hear the jingle of his belt and the rustle of his clothes, and then he climbs over me and drags the head of his cock through my juices. He rubs around my clit and my toes literally curl, arches lifting with pleasure.

"Thank you for taking care of my pussy until I got here." He shoves in with one smooth motion, burying himself deep.

I cry out, arching with the delicious pleasure of it.

"I'm going to spend the rest of the night keeping her wet and satisfied myself." He eases back then shoves in deep again.

I moan softly. Everything feels different tonight. Pavel is different—less reserved. His passion isn't so restrained and leashed. I roll my hips back to take him deeper.

He picks up speed, his breath already ragged, his need obviously as desperate as mine. He leans on one hand beside my head and holds my nape to keep me in place with the other as he rides me hard and fast.

"Pavel… Master," I gasp, already hurtling toward a finish.

"You'll come when I do," he rasps, and I can tell by his roughened voice how close he is.

"Yes!" I cry out.

He arcs in and out of me rapidly as the room spins. I want it to last forever. I need it to come to its finish. My muscles tighten around his cock.

"Don't you come without me," he warns, pumping faster.

"I won't," I promise, but it's not one I'm sure I can keep. But it doesn't matter because he's almost there. His strokes grow rough and wild, and then he shoves in deep and shouts.

I come, squeezing his cock with my inner walls in tight little pulses as the waves of bliss roll out from my core to my fingers and toes.

Pavel covers my body with his, kissing the back of my neck, his hot breath feathering over my ear. "I missed you," he says.

That's twice he's said it now. The man who communicates nothing of his own feelings with me.

I'm freefalling into love with this man who I can't have a future with. This man who lives with Sasha and is moving back to Russia.

The heartbreak when this ends is going to be exponential.

I hope I'm strong enough to withstand it.

Pavel

I bury my face in Kayla's hair and breathe in her spring flower scent. Soon, if things come together, these moments with her won't feel like stealing. Like another law I've broken. It's starting to feel possible that Kayla could truly be mine. Not just my submissive but wholly mine.

The more I let myself see the possibility of that happening, the lighter I feel.

It's crazy, this sensation of floating.

Kayla's phone rings and she moans. "Sorry, Master, I didn't turn my ringer off."

I nip her ear. "That's because you were talking to me with it," I remind her. "Do you need to check it?" I reach with my hand. It's somewhere on the bed near our knees. Finding it, I check the screen as I hand it to her. "Jagger Mason."

"Nope," she says, swiping left across the screen. I ease out of her, and she rolls over beneath me.

"Who is this man I have to kill for having your number?"

Laughter lights up her pretty face. "Oh my God, did you just make a joke?"

I toss the phone away from us. "Depends."

She keeps smiling. "He runs the promotions that we work. I already told him I couldn't work tonight. I don't know why he's calling."

"I could kill him for you," I offer.

She giggles. The musical sound enters my chest and ricochets, lighting every dark shadow there.

I smile down at her, drinking in all her sweetness.

Her phone rings again.

"I'll kill him now," I tell her, reaching for it. The screen reads, Kimberly.

"It's Kimberly. Your roommate, no?"

She frowns and reaches for the phone, so I climb off her and hand it over. She sits up, the furrow between her brows deepening as she answers the call. I go to the bathroom to wash my hands and face.

"Oh God," Kayla moans into the phone, walking toward the bathroom door. "I don't know, I mean, Pavel just got here, and he only has one night. Let me ask him."

As I dry my hands, I hear the tinny sound of Kimberly's voice from the other end of the phone. "Why do you have to ask him? Is he really that controlling? Come on, you're a grown up. You can make this decision on your own and *tell* him what you decide."

I'm not one to take criticism personally, so I wouldn't give a shit, except I see the effect of Kimberly's words on Kayla's face, and I want to punch the wall. She's gone pale, her eyes round. She appears almost sick to her stomach. Christ, does *she* think I'm too controlling?

I guess I am because I step into her space and cup her elbows. "Tell her you'll call her back," I murmur.

"I-I'll call you back," she says into the phone.

I hear Kimberly protesting, but Kayla ends the call, looking at the phone, almost as if she's frightened of it.

"What's going on?" I take the phone from her and set it on the bathroom counter.

"I guess the event they're working tonight is going to be slammed, and they need more help. Kimberly says Jagger said if I don't show up tonight, I'm fired from doing any more promotions with them." She peers up at me, as if gauging my response.

I try to gauge hers. "But you don't want to work tonight."

She spreads her hands. "Well, no. I mean, you're only here one night. This is our time together."

"So, you're not going," I say. I'm her dom, and she's looking to me to make this decision. If it helps to make me the bad guy, she can; I definitely don't give a shit.

But her expression grows more distressed. She sags. "I don't know, I don't want to let my friends down. I mean, I think one of the reasons they don't like you is because they miss me. I never work with them anymore." She blinks back tears.

"They don't like me?" Fuck, why is this the first I've heard about it? Of course, it's totally my fault. I never made the slightest attempt to ask about her roommates. Or meet them. Christ, I could have made an attempt. I've never even seen her apartment.

That suddenly strikes me as a major omission. How many others have I made?

I shake my head. "Nevermind." I hold her shoulders. "What do you want to do, Kayla? I'm a big boy, I won't sulk if you need to go to work. I can drive you there—I rented a car this time."

She gives me her big eyes. The ones that lock onto my face like I'm the god who just lit the moon. "W-would that be okay? I mean, you flew all the way out here, and now I'm ruining—"

"It's not ruined," I interrupt, brushing her hair back from her face.

Hope sparks behind her eyes. "You could hang out there—I mean, if you want. It's a private event at a night-club, but I'm sure I could get you in. Or, that would probably be boring for you—"

"Sure."

Her eyes widen in surprise. "You'd come?"

"Of course. I want to see you work."

"Great!" She's happy now. Lit up like a Christmas tree in pure, unfiltered joy. She reaches for her phone to call her roommate back.

Something I know so little about but is starting to seep in. It makes Kayla happy to get to go to work and have me come along. No, that's not it. It's about her being a pleaser. She's happy because she didn't have to disappoint me or her roommates.

I wonder if she even knows what *she* really wants.

I make it my purpose to figure that out. That's what a good dom does. That's what a *boyfriend* does.

She and Kimberly make arrangements, and she agrees to meet them at the venue in forty minutes.

I catch her with my arm around her waist as she lunges for the shower. "No, blossom. If you're going to be out serving other men tonight, I want you smelling like my cum."

Her breath catches.

I slap her bare ass. "I want my handprints on your skin and your pussy sore enough that you remember I've already been deep inside you tonight and by tomorrow morning, I'm going to turn you inside out."

She lets out a soft whimper of desire, and I nibble her ear. "I love you," I murmur.

There. I said it. It's the truth, but it was hard for me to admit out loud the first time. Now I've owned it, just like I own her.

She whirls in my arms but buries her face against my chest, like it's too intense to look at me. She bites my pect, and I full-on chuckle.

Me.

Chuckle.

Love is definitely changing me.

"Get dressed." I tell her, gently nudging her away. I give her ass another hard slap because I meant what I said about wanting my prints on her.

Not that I don't always want them there.

Soon, if I can make it all come together, she will wear those prints every fucking day and night.

15

Kayla

I get to the nightclub, which has been booked for the private event, right on time. The promotion is to get sign ups for insurance consultations, which is probably why Chuck couldn't get anyone to replace me. Personally, I think the concept is lacking. Sure, I can talk a guy into signing up because I'm cute, wear a skin-tight shirt and give him attention, but the chance of him no-showing the appointment he makes seems very high. What incentive would he have to meet them?

But that's not my problem. We get paid a flat fee plus a bonus for every appointment booked, so these stupid events can be lucrative. I'm just a thousand times grateful that Pavel was willing to come along. I don't want to be apart from him for even a minute. Not when he only has twenty-four hours in town.

Especially not when he just told me he loves me.

He loves me!

I'm still floating.

Not that it changes our circumstances. But it still makes my soul sing. Knowing he feels the same way I do.

Pavel parks his rental car in the lot, and we get out. Kimberly, Ashley, and Sheri are getting out of Ash's Cooper Mini at the same time, and Ashley waves and shouts.

I wave back and jog toward them then stop, realizing I'm being rude to Pavel.

"Sorry," I say, turning back.

"I don't need babysitting." There's an indulgence to his tone, the kind I usually only hear after he's put me through a long night of torture, and it's time for aftercare. But he's been more outwardly affectionate since he got here tonight.

It makes me feel like I could fly.

I flash him a smile and run to my friends—well, as best I can run in my high-heeled boots.

"Here's your shirt." Sheri tosses me a hot pink crop top with the insurance company's name in black letters across the tits. "I brought you a skirt, too, because I didn't know what you were wearing."

I'm in the sweater dress, so it's a good thing she brought the skirt. Except I see Pavel glowering at the short, black faux-leather mini.

He curses in Russian under his breath.

"This is Pavel," I say brightly, even though they obviously already have guessed as much. "Pavel, this is Kimberly, Ashley, and Sheri."

He shakes each of their hands, his cool, assessing gaze traveling over each of their faces. I know he heard what Kimberly said on the phone earlier about him, and I'm still cringing over it. Not that Pavel seems like the type to get hurt feelings, but I wish—I want—them to get along. But Pavel isn't like Sasha's husband Maxim—the kind who charms women with his powerful but benevolent demeanor. Pavel is Pavel—the bad boy with a dangerous air and a smile you have to work very hard to earn.

My friends may not see what I do at first.

Hopefully, they will eventually.

We go inside, and I tell Chuck I have to change but will be ready in just a few minutes. In the bathroom, I shimmy out of my sweater dress and put on the tight crop-top and miniskirt. I brush my hands down my ass, remembering the sting of Pavel's slap. The possessive words he growled in my ear about smelling like his cum.

My nipples grow hard and chafe against my bra.

Out on the floor, the room is already starting to fill. Pavel's at the bar holding a high-ball glass with a clear liquid—vodka, I assume.

It occurs to me that I don't know his favorite kind. Or even what he likes to eat, beyond room service food. There's so many things I don't know about him.

Will I ever get to learn them? Tonight, for some reason, I feel hopeful that I will. Tonight, everything feels open. Different.

I meet with Chuck to get my appointment book and assignment and head out into the crowd. It's some kind of young businessman convention—who knows what, exactly, but basically the place is packed with entitled white guys in suits, all looking like they're just out of college. By the way they're hitting the open bar, they could be still in college.

Give it a couple hours, and these guys will be handsy as hell. I've seen this sort of scene before.

I steal a glance at Pavel, pleased to find he's watching me with that intensity that sends jolts of heat to my core. I head out into the crowd, mingling with the men, chatting them up, getting their phone numbers entered into my system for appointments. Everywhere I go, the inexorable pull of Pavel's gaze follows me, an invisible connection between us that he could use to snap me back to his side with one gentle tug.

But he doesn't snap my leash. He doesn't sulk about the turn of events, even though I want to. Now that I'm here I'm angry with my decision to come. This job has been a great way to pay the rent for the last year, but it's not like it's a resume-builder or a place to meet influential people. I just felt pressured by Kimberly—maybe because she was judging my relationship with Pavel.

The fact that my roommates think I'm in an unhealthy relationship does concern me, but they also don't understand kink. Sasha gets it more, but she's pretty far from normal. She was raised in the bratva. Her father was so medieval he arranged her marriage.

When I consider things like bringing Pavel back to Wisconsin to meet my parents, it's pretty hard to imagine.

What we have is not normal.

But isn't normal overrated?

Halfway through the shift, I lose my drive. I usually work these events like I'm being graded and have to get A pluses straight down my report card, but tonight I can't see the point. These customers are asses, and the client we're working for is cheesy as hell for using hot girls to sell their stupid insurance product. It's probably some kind of swindle, anyway.

Or maybe it's just that when measuring the importance of doing this job well compared to the importance of the man patiently waiting for me at the bar, there's no comparison. Besides, I have a real job now. I went to Lara's office and signed the contract. I'm now officially a working actress. I would be quitting this job soon, anyway. I won't have time with filming the show.

The more I think about it, the more annoyed I get at

being here. Not that I'm going to walk out tonight. I have way too strong a work ethic for that. But I know now that I made the wrong choice, and Pavel and I are both paying for it.

"Hey." I hear Pavel's sharp voice, and I whirl to see some inebriated asswipe squeezing Kimberly's ass like it's dough that needs to be kneaded. Pavel leans against the bar, looking deceptively casual. "Hands off the women."

My heels click as I walk swiftly over, not that Pavel or Kimberly need back up from me.

"What are you, their pimp?" the dumbass snorts, but he has let go of Kim's ass.

"I'm the guy who's going to make you swallow your teeth if you don't apologize to her."

Kimberly's not like me. She doesn't run from confrontations. She folds her arms over her chest and cocks her head expectantly.

The guy looks from Pavel to Kimberly.

"Sorry," he says, not really sounding it.

Kimberly hip checks his table, sloshing the guy's drink into his lap. "Oops. Me too." She sashays over to where I stand beside Pavel. "Thanks," she says to Pavel then elbow nudges me. "We should bring him to all the events."

"Yeah, I think this is my last one," I tell her. "I'm not feeling it."

Kimberly blows out a breath. "Yeah, this one sucks. I'm sorry I guilted you into coming." She points a finger at Pavel. "Don't you go punishing her for this or whatever it is you do."

Beside me, Pavel goes very still.

My face flushes. "*Kimberly.*"

She shrugs. "Whatever. Consenting adults and all that." She rolls her eyes and leaves us.

"I'm sorry," I moan.

Pavel's throat works. I see that torment I saw in his eyes the night on the balcony.

"Oh God. Don't listen to her. She doesn't get it, okay? We know what we have is perfect." I press my body up against his. "It's amazing."

He's characteristically hard to read.

"I got wet when you were defending her," I murmur in his ear.

Pavel's arm loops around my back. A muscle moves in his jaw. "This has been hard for you—our relationship."

"It hasn't," I answer immediately. "It's not."

"There are consequences for lying, blossom."

He's right. It is hard—but not in the way he thinks. What's hard is the rollercoaster of closeness and cleaving. Peeling myself off the floor every Monday after he goes back home.

A home where he lives with people who know him infinitely better than I do.

What's hard is knowing it's all temporary—even what little we have. He's moving to Russia and leaving me behind.

And for some reason, that ending—which seemed far enough away when he told me, now feels like it's hurtling closer and closer. Because the more I fall in love, the more terrified I become about our inevitable end.

16

Pavel

Monday I set up an appointment with a realtor in L.A. to look at apartment buildings and spend all day researching rent prices and crunching numbers. Kayla fills my mind the entire time, but it's not the usual mental snapshots of Kayla. All the moments over the weekend where she burned my retinas with her incredible beauty.

Today, I'm thinking more about the totality of Kayla. Her friends, her career, her life. Until I saw her working that promotion and heard her roommate's judgment of our relationship, I hadn't known what I didn't know. I hadn't bothered to insert myself into Kayla's life, I'd just borrowed her from hers.

And now, I think I'm going to move to Los Angeles, and it's all going to work out fine? No, last night showed me I have some work to do. Work in areas I know jack shit about. But I'll figure it the fuck out. That's what I do.

My phone rings, and I look at the screen. I'm surprised to see it's Kayla. We don't call each other much—especially not during the day. It's usually for bedtime phone sex and a virtual tuck-in.

A bump of concern raises in my mind as I answer. "Hello beautiful."

Kayla sniffs. My fingers clench into a fist, and the hand holding the phone nearly crushes it.

"What happened?" If it's Ensign, I will kill the fucker by nightfall.

"No, no, it's nothing like that. It's just...sub drop, I think."

Fuck. We hadn't even played that hard yesterday. After sleeping in, I'd tied her up, spanked her a little. Made her come a dozen times, and then I had to head to the airport to come back here. She hadn't cried. I hadn't pushed her pain limits or endurance.

"Oh *malysh.* I wish I was there to hold you." Desperation to make those tears stop has me up and pacing around my bedroom. "Has this happened before?"

Another sniff. "Yes. Mondays are hard for me. Not usually this bad, though. That's why I called. I just needed to hear your voice."

My chest burns like my lungs are being ripped out. I had no idea she was going through this.

"Where are you?"

"In my room. I never got out of bed today. I need to get it together, though, because I'm supposed to go to the studio tonight to meet some of the cast."

"Have you eaten, blossom?"

Another sniff. "No."

"Okay. Your brain chemistry needs balancing. Get out of bed, little flower."

"Yes, sir." Her voice is still teary, but I hear her moving.

"Go and turn on the shower nice and hot." I wait until I hear the water running. "Now I want you to take a shower, get dressed and make yourself some lunch. Or breakfast. Whatever you feel like. Call me when you're done."

"Okay."

"Good girl."

"Thank you, Master."

I hang up and throw my phone at the wall. It bounces off and lands on the floor with another few bounces. I ignore it and pace around the room, stabbing my fingers through my hair.

Dammit.

I *am* bad for Kayla.

No wonder her roommates think there's something wrong with our relationship. If our time together leaves her crying and depressed afterward, it can't be right. I am no better than my father. Yes, our play may be consensual, but I'm a monster, just the same. I like to hurt the woman I love. What the fuck is wrong with me?

I pick up my phone and grab my coat. Without talking to Ravil, without telling anyone I'm leaving, I walk out.

My little slave needs me, and that's all that matters.

Kayla

I MAKE a peanut butter and jelly sandwich for myself and pour a glass of milk. Total comfort food. I sit at the table and force myself to take a bite of the sandwich then swallow the sticky bite down with a gulp of milk.

"Are you sick?" Ashley asks, coming into the kitchen.

"No." I instantly start crying again.

"Oh shit," she says, abandoning her foray into the

refrigerator to fly over to the table and sit beside me. "What's wrong? Did you and Pavel break up?"

I shake my head. "No. I just miss him."

She studies me. "This long-distance thing is tearing you apart, isn't it?"

"I don't know. Maybe. I think it's just sub-drop, though."

"What's that?"

"Well, during an intense BDSM scene, all these endorphins and feel-good chemicals dump, and you get the high from it. But sometimes it causes a big drop afterward. It takes a while for your body to reboot and balance things. Pavel's usually there to hold me and feed me a little chocolate or a meal and cuddle me until I feel better. But sometimes it hits after he's gone, and I'm just… depressed."

"Oh, baby. This isn't good, Kayla. Don't you have your first meeting at the studio tonight?"

"I know," I moan. "That's why I'm trying to get it together."

"You will," she promises, even though I see sympathy and concern bleeding through her expression. "I'm sure you will. But… you can't let this relationship affect your career. It's already taken over your life—I mean we never even see you here any more. When you are here, you're holed up in your room having phone sex with him. And this whole concept of giving over all your control to him—I just don't get it."

I stand from the table, my sandwich uneaten. Ashley might not be making me feel better, but she is pissing me off, which is better than being depressed. "I know you don't get it. None of you do, and it's making everything harder for me!" I exclaim. Yes, I may be wallowing in a bit of self-pity at the moment.

"Wait, wait. I'm sorry. I swear I'm not criticizing. I'm

just worried about you. We all are." She pulls me back, and because I'm already falling apart, I fall into her arms for a hug.

"I'm okay. I'm happy with Pavel. I know it doesn't seem that way right now, but I am. We're getting closer. It's more than just sex now. I think that may actually be why this is getting harder."

"Because he can't be your boyfriend?" she asks gently.

I bristle. "He is my boyfriend. He just can't be here. And he's moving to Russia." My shoulders sag.

"I don't know, Kay. From the outside, it really seems like this thing is hurting you."

I wipe my tears. "It's not." I draw in a terraced breath.

"Promise me something?"

"What?" I ask.

"That you'll draw a line at this affecting your career."

"It won't."

"Promise me now. If it does, you'll end things. I don't want to see you throw away everything you've worked so hard for."

"I promise." Pavel would never interfere with my career. He knows how much it means to me.

My phone on the table dings with a text, and I walk over to look at it. It's from Pavel. *I'm waiting.*

I hear the words in his dommy voice, the one that turns me aflutter. I pick up my sandwich and eat the whole thing while I stand there, not caring that Ashley's still watching me. "Pavel said I had to eat," I explain.

"Well, good," Ashley says. "I'm glad he's looking out for you."

I nod, relieved that I'd decided to call him. I didn't want to seem clingy or desperate or weird, but I also just… *needed* him. When I finish my sandwich, I gulp down the milk and call him.

"Have you eaten?" he asks.

"Yes, Master," I murmur, ducking my head and mumbling so Ashley won't hear, even though they've overheard me before.

"Good girl. How are you feeling now?"

"A little better."

"I want you to put some shoes on and get outside for a walk."

"Um, okay." I say, heading into my room to pull on a pair of sneakers. I throw on my jean jacket and head to the door. "All right, I'm heading out."

"Good. I'm going to walk with you, blossom, and I want you to tell me what you see. What's beautiful out there on your walk—besides you?"

I laugh softly, already starting to feel soothed. "Oh. Um… okay. Well, right now I'm in the elevator."

"What's beautiful?"

What's beautiful… in an elevator? I look around, seeing it with a new lens. "Well, it's clean. Pretty basic. But it always runs well. It smells like lemons."

"Like lemons?"

"Yeah. Must be the cleaner. But it's nice." The elevator doors open, and I walk outside. "There's a palm tree in front of my building, and it dropped some of its bark. I stop over the piece of bark and stare down at it. "It's in the shape of a heart." I tilt my head. "Actually, it kind of looks like a bodice that's been ripped open by a lover."

"Mmm. A rough lover."

"Yes." I walk on, looking around for something else to report. I notice the concrete planter boxes at the end of the sidewalk and walk over to examine the plants there.

"You like it rough, *malysh*?"

"Yes." I finger the green striped leaf of the trailing plant that grows inside, contrasting with the purple leaves of a wandering Jew. I walk on, looking at a woman pushing a stroller across the street. "I see a toddler with pink pants and kicking feet," I report. "And tiny Crocs on her feet."

"Hmm. What else?"

"A jacaranda tree. My favorite."

"What does it look like?

"It has beautiful purple flowers. They're in bloom now."

We continue on our walk, me seeking out and naming all the beautiful things in my neighborhood, until I loop back around the block in front of my place.

"How do you feel now, blossom?"

"Better," I say. It's true. I do. I'm calm and steady now. The act of looking for beauty, or maybe just noticing the world around me instead of the turmoil inside, brought me peace. I may not be my usual Energizer Bunny self, but I certainly feel grounded.

"What time do you need to go to the studio?"

"Not until this evening. They're filming today but wanted me to stop by for a cast meeting at six."

"What can you do to make yourself feel good this afternoon?"

I lean into the question to feel for an answer. "I think I'll go get groceries. And maybe clean my room."

"Would that make you feel better?"

"Yes."

"All right. Text me when you're finished with those things."

A puff of warmth fills my chest. "I will. Pavel?"

"Yes, little flower?"

"Thank you."

"*YA lyublyu vas.*"

"What's that mean?"

"I love you." He ends the call before I can respond. I hold the phone to my chest, eyes filling with tears.

This can't be wrong, what we have together.

I know it's not wrong.

Pavel

Where are you, Pavel? You are in deep shit with me.

I ignore Ravil's text and ring the bell of Kayla's fourth floor apartment. I should have visited her in her own apartment before today. That fact makes me grit my teeth with self-disgust as I wait for an answer. It's yet another indicator that I am ill-equipped to be a boyfriend.

Kimberly answers, and she's not impressed with my arrival. Not that I expected her to be. She cocks a hip and surveys me, tossing her long dark hair over one shoulder. "Dude, she does not need this distraction right now."

I push past her and into their living room, looking around at the cluttered but friendly space.

"You know she's supposed to go to the studio tonight, right? For her new part?"

I ignore her. "Kayla." I don't raise my voice, don't put a question mark on the end. That's not my style.

A door bursts open. "Pavel!"

The two seconds it takes her to sprint across the room and wrap those slender legs around my waist take all the oxygen from the room. I squeeze her tight, closing my eyes and breathing in her spring meadow scent.

"Blossom," I murmur.

"What are you doing here?"

"I had to make sure you were okay. Are you?"

She lifts her face from where it's buried in my neck. "I am now."

"Thank fuck." I walk her back into her bedroom and kick the door shut behind us. "Let me see you." I lay her on the bed. She looks like a goddess with her hair curled in soft waves and make-up that gives her a fresh dewy look. "You look beautiful, blossom. Are you ready for your meeting tonight?" I try to lower her to her feet, but she keeps clinging to me like a koala bear. So damn adorable.

"Yes."

"How long do you have before you have to leave?"

"Long enough for you to remind me who I belong to."

I chuckle. An honest-to-goodness laugh. Because those words are like music to my ears. But I'm not going to dominate her today. She's had enough of that. This afternoon I'm going to do something I've never done before—make love to her.

I kick off my shoes and climb over her, melding my mouth to hers. "You already know who you belong to," I whisper, lightly wrapping my hand around her throat, my thumb caressing the front of it. "Don't you?"

"Yes, Master."

"I don't need to remind you." I lay a trail of kisses down the side of her neck and across her collarbone to the hollow at the base of her throat. "I need to reward you."

She lets out a soft sigh as I slide a hand under her shirt and bra to cup her breast. I lightly thumb her nipple. "I haven't rewarded you enough, have I?"

She makes a little humming sound.

I tug her shirt off over her head and unsnap her bra in the back. "Have I, blossom?"

"I-I don't know."

"What kind of rewards do you like?" I unbutton her skinny jeans and slide them off her legs then grasp the sides of her panties and lay a kiss on her mound before I start to slowly draw them down.

"You." She reaches her fingertips down to graze mine before I'm out of her reach. "Just you, Pavel."

I toss the panties on the floor with the other clothes and slide my hands behind her knees to lift them. "So spa time misses the mark."

"I liked that, too. I like everything you do."

"Not *everything*," I challenge as I lower my head between her legs and lick into her.

She gasps, legs squeezing around my shoulders, pelvis shooting up off the bed. I pin her down and slowly trail the tip of my tongue around the insides of her labia.

"Everything," she insists. It's a lie, but I'll let her believe it for the moment. It's her fantasy, why poke holes in it?

I find her clit and circle it with my tongue, then use my finger to rub it as I move up to suck her nipple. "How do you want to come, little flower?" I ask as I leave one nipple to suck the other. "On my fingers? On my tongue?" I don't usually leave these choices up to her—that's part of our game, but today I want to be the one to serve. Hearing her crying this morning ripped a hole in the fabric with which I've woven this fantasy of ours. The need to fix what I've done, to heal what's torn is more important to me than anything. Today, I only want to pleasure my beautiful slave, to make her feel good.

"On your cock, Master."

"You need me inside you?"

"Yes, please?"

I delay my own pleasure, stroking and kissing every inch of her skin before I finally free my rock hard erection and give her what she needs. What we both need.

When it's over, I shower her with more kisses, then get a damp washcloth to clean her up. "Feel better, little flower?"

"Yes. Much better."

"Good. Let's get you ready for your meeting at the studio. Can I drive you there? What can I do to help?"

She climbs off the bed and accepts the clothing I hand her, piece by piece from the floor. "Are you staying the night?"

I hesitate, my phone with Ravil's text smoking up my phone. I need to square things away with him—find out his terms for letting me move. Then I can be with Kayla full time. We won't have the violence of ripping apart and stitching ourselves back together week after week. "I'll see if I can. I will stay until after your meeting for certain. I know there's a late flight out of here."

"Yay," she says softly, pulling on the designer jeans and pretty shirt.

"Now, what about food?" I tip my head to the door. "May I take you out?"

Her smile could light a stadium at night. "Yes. We'll have to keep it short, but that would be perfect. Then you could drop me off at the studio."

Ravil can wait. Right now, all that matters is Kayla.

17

Kayla

A young, beautiful studio assistant with huge black-framed glasses and a high ponytail picks me up from the front lobby and escorts me back through the giant building that must be at least eight thousand square feet. The director of *Bad Boys* is Lottie James, a gorgeous African American woman who radiates both warmth and power.

"It's such an honor to meet you. Thank you so much for this opportunity," I gush. "I cannot tell you how big a fan I am of the show. *Huge*. I'm sorry—I was going to try to bury the fangirl tonight."

Ms. James gives me a broad smile. "No, please." She beckons with both hands. "Tell me more. I love this show, too."

"Well, you're doing everything right. It's smart, it's sexy, it's fun. The fact that it's already a cult favorite speaks volumes."

"I was kidding, but thank you." Lottie winks at me. "I like you already, Kayla. Okay, Jenny will give you a tour and introduce you to the cast. They are all coming off a long day of filming, so don't take it personally if they don't stay for more than a minute." She breezes out, leaving me with Jenny.

"Thank you. I won't. Again, I'm thrilled to meet you," I call to her departing back.

Jenny shows me around the space, pointing out the different sets and the dressing rooms and makeup. I meet the costume crew, the tech crew, and finally each of the actors.

Ms. James was right, no one has a lot of time for me, but everyone is friendly and welcoming. A half hour later, I'm back outside in the parking lot, waiting for Pavel to pick me up. It all seems too easy. Too perfect.

I should have known that nothing in this industry works like that.

I should have known that pretty little not-special actors like me don't get handed parts out like it's a high school musical.

"Looking forward to seeing you on set," the lead bad boy actor, Brad Lowell says as he walks out with two of the other actors.

"Thank you so much!" I call out.

"So what part is she playing again?" Ryanna Jones asks him as they walk away.

"I don't know. I guess they created a part for her. She's Blake Ensign's niece or something."

Blake Ensign's niece.

Oh God.

Oh my fucking God.

I didn't get this part. It wasn't my fantastic audition or my post-play openness or my talent that got me here.

It was Pavel's fists.

Or his gun.

God, I don't even know what he did to get me this part.

Tears blur my eyes as I start speed-walking in my heels and skinny jeans out of the parking lot. I don't know where I'm going, all I know is that I need to leave. I can't be here when Pavel arrives. I don't want to be anywhere near him or this studio at this moment.

I wish the pavement would crack open and swallow me down.

I sense rather than see a car pull up beside me.

"*Kayla.*" Pavel's deep voice holds alarm.

When I keep walking, the tires screech. I still don't look. I can't do this right now.

I just. Can't.

A door slams and then Pavel catches me around the waist. "Hold up. Kayla, what happened?" There's a dangerous edge to his voice, but I know by now it's not for me.

I turn and try to shove at his chest. "You happened!" I shout then look around, realizing that making a scene in the parking lot is not going to win me any more points around here. I turn and try to walk away again, but Pavel catches me again, pulling me by the waist until my back hits his front.

"Hold up." His voice is soft in my ear. This man never raises his voice. It's part of that perfect dommy charm, but right now, it infuriates me.

"Let go of me."

"I'm sorry."

"Oh, so you do know what you did?"

He holds me tight but is still. "What happened?"

"You told me we didn't lie to each other. You asked for my honesty, but you didn't give me yours."

"I didn't lie. I've never lied to you."

"You let me believe I got this job based on a *good audi-*

tion. You didn't tell me because you knew I wouldn't like it, Pavel."

"Kayla, he *offered*. We were sweating him, and he threw a job for you in the ring. How could I turn that down? You've told me your dreams, *malysh*. How could I possibly block an opportunity?"

"Let go of me."

Pavel's arm around me loosens slowly then eventually gives way, and I spin to face him. "It was wrong, Pavel. Beating him up—or whatever you did was wrong. That's not the way normal people do business." It's a low blow considering I pretty much sanctioned it at the time, but everything seems different now. "I don't want a job that I got because of my connection to the Russian mob. I wanted a job because I was good enough."

Pavel spreads his hands. "You *are* good enough, blossom. You're twenty times over good enough."

I scoff and shake my head. "How would you know? You've never even seen me perform."

"I just know." He sounds so sure.

"No. You know absolutely nothing about my career."

And that's when Ashley's words come back to me. The promise I made to her.

This relationship *is* interfering with my career. Big time.

It's definitely clouded my whole life. Turned me upside down and inside out. And my career is far too important to me, far too fragile for me to not have my head in the game.

"I'm calling red on us." The moment I speak the words, everything in me goes dead. Like the soundtrack to my life suddenly got cut off. "I can't do this anymore."

Pavel shoves his hands in his pockets. He doesn't speak.

"You said when I was done, you'd let me go."

Pavel's throat bobs. "Of course." His voice comes out raspy and hoarse. "Let me drive you home."

I want to refuse—to schedule a rideshare instead—but it's dark out, and I know Pavel won't leave me here alone. I nod, ignoring the tear that skates down my cheek.

A cocoon of pain wraps me on the drive home. White noise blaring in my ears, heaviness pushing against my chest. Neither of us speaks.

Pavel pulls up in front of my apartment and starts to get out.

"Let me go." I'm surprised at how clear and firm I sound.

He shuts his door again.

I throw mine open and get out. "Goodbye, Pavel."

He's looking straight ahead, both hands on the wheel. He doesn't answer. As I close the door, I see his lips move and hear the murmur of something soft in Russian.

Later, I would wish I'd listened. Asked him to translate. But by then, it was too late. He was long gone. He set me free as he promised, and he wasn't coming back.

18

Pavel

It takes my housemates a couple days to notice that the lights are out inside my head. I'm still eating. Still speaking although not much.

It wouldn't be hard to argue that I was dead inside before I met Kayla. Now, there's no doubt. I don't allow myself to think. Or to feel. Or to do anything but the most mechanical of actions.

After I dropped Kayla off that night, I returned the rental car. Flew back to Chicago.

Found Ravil and told him I was staying. And then I went out on the roof to let the cold bite of an April night soak into my bones. Freezing all my organs exactly in place.

It's not until Sasha asks me how the apartment building hunting is going that anything even moves in my chest.

Not that my heart flopping like a fish on land is anything worth celebrating.

"The deal is off," I tell her, without looking away from the television we are all gathered around.

She hits pause on the *Game of Thrones* episode. "Wait… what?"

Dima looks over from his work station, stopping his usual incessant clacking of keys.

"Turn it back on." I lift my chin toward the television like I actually care about some dragon queen.

"Oh my God, what happened?" Sasha gasps.

Now everyone looks—Nikolai, Oleg, Story, Maxim. Apparently Ravil hadn't shared my failure with the rest of the suite.

"Did she break up with you? She found out about the part, didn't she?"

The pain I hadn't allowed myself to feel seeps in through the cuts Sasha makes.

"Turn it back on."

Maxim leans forward, resting his elbows on his knees.

"I'm sorry, Pavel," Story says softly. Oleg circles his fist over his chest in the sign for *sorry*.

"Wait—what Kayla ended things? Is that why you flew back there Monday?"

I shake my head, shocked by the pain in my chest, my ribs, my gut. "I was wrong for her. It was a bad idea to move out there, anyway. This is for the best."

Sasha stands and throws her hands out. "So what, you're not going to fight for her? You quit just like that? Well, damn, I'm glad I didn't go into business with you if that's how you approach challenges."

"Sasha," Maxim warns.

"Pavel doesn't quit," Dima says quietly from his work station. "He's stubborn as hell."

"I don't keep my women against their will, unlike you *mudaks,*" I snap.

Maxim straightens, probably offended, since he kept his bride prisoner here until he tamed her. So did Ravil.

"There's a pretty large area between keeping a woman captive and trying to work things out," Nikolai counters.

I shake my head. "No. It wasn't a good match to begin with. It's better this way."

"Really, dude? Because you both seemed pretty smitten when I saw you two together," Dima says.

Fresh pain rips through my chest, so sharp I can barely breathe.

"Pavel, give her some time, but don't give up. She's mad that you interfered, right?"

I drop my head into my hands. "It's more than that, Sasha." The sound of Kayla's hiccuping voice over the phone replays in my head, and I'm suddenly bone tired. "That's why I won't fight for her." I get up and stalk to the penthouse door to go to my room across the hall. "And don't interfere," I warn, turning back and pointing a finger at Sasha.

"You're an asshole, Pavel," Sasha calls as I shut the door.

No argument here. I stalk to my room and stand at the window that overlooks the city. I'm definitely an asshole. Why I thought I could navigate a relationship when I literally know nothing about keeping a woman happy is beyond me.

All I know how to do is hurt people. That is literally what I do for a living. What I did for Kayla. What we had wasn't wrong, but it wasn't right, either. I don't know how to love. How to heal the scars this life has given me. I thought maybe I could with Kayla, but that was just a fantasy.

Maybe if I'd learned faster. If I'd talked more. If only I'd told her sooner that I planned to move out there with her, maybe we'd have a more solid base when I broke her trust. Maybe she wouldn't have fallen so hard when I left at the end of the weekend. A submissive needs to feel safe, but I didn't give her much to hold onto. It's no wonder her roommates didn't like the relationship. It's no wonder she threw in the towel at the first bump in the road.

One thing I do know now—me moving back to Russia wouldn't fix anything for my mom, either. I'm too broken to heal her. She doesn't need my physical protection anymore. No one's coming after her but her own shadows. She needs help from people who do know how to love. How to give and share and be happy.

I get on my phone and book a ticket. I'm going to go back to Russia to get her and bring her back here to the Kremlin. It's one thing I can do that might be right.

~

Kayla

On Saturday the surge of righteousness and determination I rode since my break-up dissolves, and I'm left gutted and empty. The knowledge that Pavel won't be coming this weekend, or any weekend in the future, unravels the last bit of certainty I had that I was doing the right thing.

I force myself to get out of the house for fear I'd stay in bed all day, but of course, when I set off on a walk, all I can think of is the incredible sweetness of Pavel coaxing me outside to look for beautiful things.

I try it for myself now to combat the approaching tears.

The only problem is that everything beautiful I see I want to report back to him.

My phone rings, and I jerk it out of my pocket. Not because I hope it's Pavel. I know better than to hope that. He made it clear he would let me go when I asked him to.

It's Sasha. She's been calling for the last few days, but I haven't taken her calls. I haven't even listened to her messages because I didn't want her to change my mind.

Now though?

It's already changing.

I answer. "Hey, you." I sound ancient. Tired.

"Kayla, what the hell? Are you okay? Why haven't you called me back?"

I want to ask about Pavel. A million things. But I can't. So instead, I squeeze my eyes closed to keep the tears from coming out.

"Are you okay?" Sasha's voice is quieter. "What happened? Please talk to me. I'm so worried."

"Did you know?" I ask, tears clogging my throat.

"That you broke up? Yes."

"No, about the part. Did you know?"

"Oh. Well, I suspected, yes. I mean, he is Pavel. He makes men piss themselves and weep for their mothers."

"Did he tell you what they did?" my voice raises. I don't know why I'm mad at Sasha right now, but I am.

"No, of course not," she says immediately. "They don't tell me anything. That would make me an accessory."

The green-eyed monster settles down.

"How could I be so naive? I thought I got that part on my own."

"Who cares how you got the part, Kayla?" Sasha protests. "It's always who you know in show business. You know that. That's why you've been working those promotions—hoping to get out there and meet the right people. Well, the right person got behind you this time. It doesn't matter why."

"It does matter. I thought I was good enough to do this, and now..." —I choke back a sob— "...now, I know I'm not."

"Bologna," Sasha says, making the word sound cute in her accent. "You are good enough. Pavel got you the part, now you do the rest. Show them how great you are. Get yourself the next part all on your own. *Don't you dare* walk away from that part, or I will fly over there and kick your ass myself."

"I wasn't going to walk away from it," I sniff. "I wanted to be that proud, but I couldn't bring myself to make that call." I think of the other call I've been burning to make. "I think I overreacted with Pavel."

"You did. I mean, I'm sure there are many things I don't understand about your relationship, but I do know the guy was ready to move out there to be with you. I mean, he was head over heels in love, Kayla. I don't see why you'd throw that away so easily."

My knees go weak, and I drop onto a park bench. "He was ready to move out here?"

"Yes! We were going to finance his real estate venture out there. He was working on a plan."

Hope skids across my chest and then flares to life like a match strike. All the desperation that's crowded in this week starts to lift.

He was going to move here. He wanted to be with me full time.

And I ended things. Oh God, I made such a terrible mistake. The totality of it comes crashing down on me from every side.

"I gotta go, Sasha." I rise to my feet, a surge of adrenaline suddenly running through me. "Thanks for calling." I hang up before she can answer and dial Pavel as I walk swiftly toward my apartment.

He doesn't answer.

Dammit.

I end the call, then change my mind and call back to leave a message.

"Pavel?" I croak into the phone. I've reached the front of my apartment building, and I stand in front of the planter I'd never noticed until he made me look for beautiful things.

That's the thing with relationships, too. Just like life. Whatever you look for, is what you see. When you look for beauty, you find it. When you look for problems, you can discover those, too. What Pavel and I had was something unusual. Special.

I finger one of the leaves now. "I'm sorry. I, um, I probably overreacted about the part. Can we talk?" I hang up, my heart pounding.

I go up to my apartment, which I thankfully have to myself for once. I pace around the living room for the next hour, but he doesn't return my call.

Gah.

What do I do now? I send the same message as a text.

Still no reply.

I wait another hour and try to call again, knowing I'm acting desperate and not caring. Hell, I am desperate.

I threw away my relationship with Pavel because it wasn't normal. It didn't fit in a pretty box that could be tied up with a bow. It wasn't a romance novel relationship. My friends didn't understand it. It challenged my moral compass.

None of that has changed. I don't know how to fix all those things. But what I do know is that I want it back. I want Pavel in my life. I want to soften his edges and draw strength from his hardness. I want him in my corner, backing me up, protecting me, making me swoon with his soft, dommy commands.

Pavel doesn't answer, so I try leaving another message.

"Pavel?" I can't stop the tears, and I don't try. "I'm sorry I ended things. Please, can we talk? I was so muddled; I had sub-drop that day, so my emotions were out of whack, and Sheri had made me promise that morning not to let the relationship interfere with my career, so I guess when it did, I just overreacted. Can you call me back, please?"

He still doesn't return my call.

I try seven more times, and finally, at midnight Chicago time, I text Sasha to ask if Pavel's around.

Her reply shreds me: *He's gone. He went to Russia.*

I sink to the floor and sob.

I lost him.

I had him—he was going to move here to be with me—and I ruined it. He was so sure he was bad for me that the moment I agreed, he backed off. He backed off so far, he left the country.

I drop my forehead to my knees and cry for the man who holds my heart. The man I love.

The man I lost.

19

Pavel

When I arrive back in the States with my mother, I see all the messages from Kayla, but I don't listen to them. I can't bear to.

I knew her well enough to suspect she'd be back in touch once the anger wore off. A pleaser like her doesn't like discord. Ending things the way we did wouldn't sit right with her. She would reach back out for closure.

And my plan is to give her exactly what she needs. To set her free emotionally. To tell her I care about her. Wish her well. Pledge my protection and assistance if she ever needs it in the future.

But I'm putting off that conversation because the burn of losing her is like an acid eating me from the inside out. I can't stop obsessing over her. Remembering every single moment we spent together. Seeing all the places I could have treated her better. Shared more. Let her in.

She wanted to come to Chicago. I should have invited her. She wanted to know me better; she was jealous of

Sasha's proximity. I should have made sure she never felt jealous again. That she held all my most sacred secrets.

Most of all, I regret not telling her what she meant to me. That I wanted to keep her—permanently. I keep wondering if it would have made a difference. Probably not, but I'm second guessing.

I get my mom settled in a one-bedroom in the Kremlin and introduce her to Svetlana, the midwife and her daughter, Natasha, the massage therapist. Svetlana is well-respected in the building and promised to introduce my mother to everyone and make sure she settles in. Surprisingly, this is the happiest I've seen my mother. Ever. I think she really bought into the new start thing once we packed up her shit and left her place. She's seemed hopeful ever since.

When I get up to the penthouse, I'm stupid with jetlag and exhaustion.

Natasha comes out of Dima's room, blushing. I'd be happy the asshole finally hooked up with her, but I'm too dead to feel anything.

I walk into the kitchen to raid the refrigerator, and Sasha launches herself from the couch and comes at me.

"What in the hell is wrong with you?" she demands. She stalks into the kitchen and gets right up into my face. "Kayla is *suffering*, and you won't even call her back." She points a finger in my face.

I catch her wrist. "What do you mean, suffering?" I demand, alarm sharpening my exhausted brain.

Maxim enters the kitchen and stands behind Sasha. "Let go of my wife," he growls.

I release Sasha before I get punched in the face.

"Ashley called me to say she won't get out of bed. She hasn't eaten. She cries all the time." Sasha gives my chest a poke. "*I told you not to hurt her.*"

The alarms in my head have turned to full sirens.

I can only stare at my furious suitemate as the thoughts connect and disconnect in my head. And then I'm out the door and heading for the airport.

Kayla

After Sheri, Ashley, and Kimberly forced me out of bed and into the shower, I left the apartment to go on a drive to be alone.

Last night when they tried to get me to eat by plying me with ice cream, I broke down and told them the whole story—about what Blake Ensign did. Pavel's solution. The part I got as a result. How I broke up with him and then later found out he was planning to move here to be with me.

If I weren't so depressed, I would have a bitter laugh over the irony that they turned Team Pavel after hearing the story.

At least we're all in agreement that I fucked up.

I don't have a destination in mind, but I find myself down at the pier. My thinking place. The place I go when I'm ready to give up.

I guess that means subconsciously I don't want to give up on my relationship with Pavel. And yet, I have to. I find a place to park and walk down to the end of the pier. A bench is open, and I plop down onto it.

I listen to the sound of the waves and the seagulls. The din of voices around me. My face grows wet with quiet tears.

Breaking you was always my worst fear, Blossom.

I hear Pavel's voice in my head and lean into the sound.

What is he saying?

The person on the bench beside me reaches out to touch my shoulder, and I jerk my head up to tell them I'm fine.

"Pavel?" I wipe my tears, blinking rapidly. "You're here?"

He picks up my hand and pulls it to his lips. "I'm here, beautiful."

"Are you taking me back?" I realize how pathetic and desperate I sound. "I'm sorry--I… what are you doing here?"

"Come here." He reaches for my waist and pulls me to straddle his lap, my shins resting on the bench, my arms tangled around his neck. "I told you I wouldn't lie to you, Kayla, but I did. I lied when I said I'd let you go." He shakes his head. "You're mine, blossom. Nothing can change that."

"I thought…" The lack of food and sleep in the past week is doing a number on my brain. I can't seem to understand what's happening. "Did you move to Russia?"

"No, little flower. I moved my mother to Chicago. I'm sorry, my phone was off the entire time I was there, and I didn't get your messages until today."

"You moved your mother…" I clap a hand over my mouth and laugh hysterically. "I thought you were gone forever."

"I intended to stay away, beautiful, but I just can't. I meant it when I said you're everything to me. There's just no reason to exist except for you."

"Pavel." I choke on a sob and strangle him with my hug.

He rubs my back and presses a kiss on my neck.

"I was wrong to doubt us. I love you, Pavel. I'm scared by how much I need you, but rejecting your help where I most needed it was cutting off my nose to spite my face. The truth is, I don't even care about my career anymore. You're what's important to me."

"No," he says sharply. "I won't allow that. Your career comes first. That's why I'm moving here, so I can support you better."

Now I cry like a baby. "I want you here," I agree. "I really want that."

"You'll have it. You'll have everything you want from me. I promise."

"I don't want safe words for this relationship," I tell him.

He arches a brow.

"No exits. No outs. Neither of us gets to call *red*."

His lips slowly stretch into a smile. "I won't let you go again, little flower. You belong to me, and I'll never release you. Not even in death."

I kiss him. "Promise?"

His gaze is a warm caress on my face. "I promise," he murmurs.

EPILOGUE

Pavel

We close on the apartment building on a beautiful June day. Sasha and Kayla both look like movie stars in their short shorts, high heels, and sunglasses snapping a selfie in front of it for Sasha's Instagram. I stand back and watch, hardly believing it's all real. That it happened so easily.

That's what life with Kayla is like—easy. She makes me feel like a god with her total surrender, her belief in me, her bright, happy smiles any time I'm near.

Maxim stands beside me, his gaze on Sasha soft.

"Thank you, brother. I still can't believe you did this for me."

"It's a worthwhile investment," Maxim says. "And you're family."

Family.

In the bratva, we are supposed to break all ties to our former families and swear allegiance only to the brotherhood. That's one of the reasons I was sent away for killing my father. I wasn't supposed to be looking in on my mother any more.

Until Kayla cracked open my blackened heart, I didn't allow myself to truly acknowledge or receive the benefits of brotherhood. Of men who would do anything for me--not just kill or die, but shape me, mold me, and launch me back into the world with an opportunity to make something more of myself.

I'm humbled by the support they've given me--all of them.

Ravil's terms were easy. I still belong to him. When he needs something, I'll do it. For the moment, he hasn't made any requests, but when he does, I won't balk. I won't hesitate to serve the *pahkan* who deserves all my respect and honor.

"Let's go open this bottle of Dom Perignon," Sasha says, holding up the bottle clutched in her fist and waving two glasses with the other hand.

Maxim holds up the two he was tasked with carrying. "Right behind you," he says.

"Wait, wait!" I call, jogging forward.

The women stare at me like I have two heads. I reach Kayla and scoop her up into a honeymoon carry. "Isn't this how you do it?" I ask, carrying her through the doorway.

She giggles and kisses my neck. "Thank you, Master," she purrs in my ear.

I try to will away the boner that breathy honorific gives me.

We take the elevator to the rooftop because all the units are currently rented, a condition we don't want to mess with for the moment. Next month Kayla and I will be able to move into the penthouse suite and start remodeling it, but for now, the cash generated from rent will go into the building upgrades. Maxim and Sasha own the building outright and aren't requiring me to pay a cent toward that expense. I'll manage the property and upgrades and split the profits from it with them. If or when they choose to sell it, they'll split the gains with me. Maxim and I did a gentleman's handshake on the deal because we're bratva brothers. Brothers don't solve things in courts. If something goes wrong, the grievance will be dealt with in blood. To me, this means nothing will go wrong. We deal in honor, and both of us will honor our commitments.

I don't put Kayla down, not until we're out on the rooftop. "Welcome to our new home," I say.

She lifts her lips for a kiss. "You did this," she murmurs. "You make impossible things possible."

My chest grows tight and my eyes burn for a moment. I know she's talking about the part, too, which she's forgiven me for. She's been filming for the show and finding her place in a new and exciting world at the studio.

"You," is all I can say. I can hardly take how beautiful she looks with those eyes shining up at me, the California sun sparkling over the pool behind her.

Maxim pops the cork on the champagne, drawing us from our intimate moment. He pours four glasses and hands them around.

"To Pavel and Kayla," Sasha says. "Keep her happy, or you're a dead man."

I clink glasses with Kayla, drinking in the gift of her adoring gaze. "She's my reason for living," I murmur.

Kayla's lips part and she draws in a shaky breath. "He is my happiness," she murmurs back, neither of us breaking our locked gaze.

"Aw," Sasha says, and I hear the sound of her kissing Maxim.

I loop my arm around Kayla and draw her up against me. "To Maxim and Sasha. Thank you for believing in me enough to make this new venture possible."

"Yes, to Maxim and Sasha," Kayla repeats warmly.

All four of us clink glasses together and then drain them.

"Group hug," Sasha calls.

I roll my eyes, because I'm the last guy who would ever join a group hug, but Kayla propels me forward and we join arms in a circle, the ladies laughing and jostling us around.

"I love you guys," Sasha says as we break apart.

I can't say it back, because my throat closes, but Kayla squeezes my waist. "We love you, too. Thank you so much for everything."

We walk to the edge of the rooftop as a group and watch the sun lower in the sky until the giant ball paints the sky in red, pink and orange.

I press against Kayla's back and breath in her spring meadow scent, humbled by how much beauty is in my life.

Thank you for reading The Soldier. If you enjoyed it, please consider leaving a review—they make such a difference for indie authors. For a special bonus epilogue featuring the premiere of Kayla's television series, be sure to join Renee's mailing list. Stay tuned for Dima's story next—I have all kinds of surprises in store for him and his twin.

WANT FREE RENEE ROSE BOOKS?

Go to http://subscribepage.com/alphastemp to sign up for Renee Rose's newsletter and receive a free copy of *Alpha's Temptation, Theirs to Protect, Owned by the Marine, Theirs to Punish, The Alpha's Punishment, Disobedience at the*

Dressmaker's and *Her Billionaire Boss*. In addition to the free stories, you will also get special pricing, exclusive previews and news of new releases.

OTHER TITLES BY RENEE ROSE

Chicago Bratva

"Prelude" in Black Light: Roulette War

The Director

The Fixer

"Owned" in Black Light: Roulette Rematch

The Enforcer

The Soldier

The Hacker

Vegas Underground Mafia Romance

King of Diamonds

Mafia Daddy

Jack of Spades

Ace of Hearts

Joker's Wild

His Queen of Clubs

Dead Man's Hand

Wild Card

More Mafia Romance

Her Russian Master

Contemporary

Daddy Rules Series

Fire Daddy

Hollywood Daddy

Stepbrother Daddy

Master Me Series

Her Royal Master

Her Russian Master

Her Marine Master

Yes, Doctor

Double Doms Series

Theirs to Punish

Theirs to Protect

Holiday Feel-Good

Scoring with Santa

Saved

Other Contemporary

Black Light: Valentine Roulette

Black Light: Roulette Redux

Black Light: Celebrity Roulette

Black Light: Roulette War

Black Light: Roulette Rematch

Punishing Portia (written as Darling Adams)

The Professor's Girl

Safe in his Arms

Paranormal

Two Marks Series

Tempted

Wolf Ranch Series

Rough

Wild

Feral

Savage

Fierce

Ruthless

Wolf Ridge High Series

Alpha Bully

Alpha Knight

Bad Boy Alphas Series

Alpha's Temptation

Alpha's Danger

Alpha's Prize

Alpha's Challenge

Alpha's Obsession

Alpha's Desire

Alpha's War

Alpha's Mission

Alpha's Bane

Alpha's Secret

Alpha's Prey

Alpha's Sun

Shifter Ops

Alpha's Moon

Alpha's Vow

Alpha's Revenge

Midnight Doms

Alpha's Blood

His Captive Mortal

Alpha Doms Series

The Alpha's Hunger

The Alpha's Promise

The Alpha's Punishment

Other Paranormal

The Winter Storm: An Ever After Chronicle

Sci-Fi

Zandian Masters Series

His Human Slave

His Human Prisoner

Training His Human

His Human Rebel

His Human Vessel

His Mate and Master

Zandian Pet

Their Zandian Mate

His Human Possession

Zandian Brides

Night of the Zandians

Bought by the Zandians

Mastered by the Zandians

Zandian Lights

Kept by the Zandian

Claimed by the Zandian

Stolen by the Zandian

Other Sci-Fi

The Hand of Vengeance

Her Alien Masters

Regency

The Darlington Incident

Humbled

The Reddington Scandal

The Westerfield Affair

Pleasing the Colonel

Western

His Little Lapis

The Devil of Whiskey Row

The Outlaw's Bride

Medieval

Mercenary

Medieval Discipline

Lords and Ladies

The Knight's Prisoner

Betrothed

Held for Ransom

The Knight's Seduction

The Conquered Brides (5 book box set)

Renaissance

Renaissance Discipline

ABOUT RENEE ROSE

USA TODAY BESTSELLING AUTHOR RENEE ROSE loves a dominant, dirty-talking alpha hero! She's sold over a million copies of steamy romance with varying levels of kink. Her books have been featured in USA Today's *Happily Ever After* and *Popsugar*. Named Eroticon USA's Next Top Erotic Author in 2013, she has also won *Spunky and Sassy's* Favorite Sci-Fi and Anthology author, *The Romance Reviews* Best Historical Romance, and *has* hit the *USA Today* list eight times with her Bad Boy Alpha and Wolf Ranch series, as well as various anthologies.

Please follow her on:
Bookbub | Goodreads | Tiktok

Renee loves to connect with readers!
www.reneeroseromance.com
reneeroseauthor@gmail.com

Printed in the USA
CPSIA information can be obtained
at www.ICGtesting.com
CBHW021527010324
4848CB00040B/710